I0668028

Blanca Is My Name

Or How I Saved the Buffalo on the Texas Plains

PRESTON LEWIS

ILLUSTRATIONS BY JASON C. ECKHARDT

EAKIN PRESS ⚑ Fort Worth, Texas
www.EakinPress.com

Copyright © 2002
By Preston Lewis
Published By Eakin Press
An Imprint of Wild Horse Media Group
P.O. Box 331779
Fort Worth, Texas 76163
1-817-344-7036
www.EakinPress.com
ALL RIGHTS RESERVED
1 2 3 4 5 6 7 8 9
ISBN-10: 0-9771610-8-0
ISBN-13: 978-0-9771610-8-9

In Grateful Memory of
Ed Eakin
1927–2002
A Friend of Texas Letters

Contents

The Mystery of the "White Buffalo Diary"

Shortly after my book *They Call Me Old Blue* appeared, I received a call from Suzanne Campbell with a curious proposition. Suzanne, head of the Dr. Ralph R. Chase West Texas Collection at Angelo State University, said the collection had some papers I might like to examine.

Those familiar with *They Call Me Old Blue* will remember that the book was based on a series of papers purporting to be the memoirs of Old Blue. Old Blue, as you may recall, was Texas pioneer rancher Charles Goodnight's famed lead steer. While those papers could not be conclusively proven to be the memoirs of Old Blue, neither could they be so easily disproved. So, I typed up the handwritten story of Old Blue, edited it, and found a publisher in Eakin Press in Austin.

Because I had had experience dealing with manuscripts supposedly of animal origin, Suzanne approached me about a set of early recollections staff members had found when they moved into new quarters in the fall of 2000. She pulled one of the boxes from the closed stacks and opened it for me. Inside was a large padded envelope, and inside that were two more mailing envelopes. Inside the last was a narrow ledger of a style used before the turn of the twentieth century.

I could not fathom why Suzanne had called me over to inspect financial records. She knew I liked good stories rather than numbers. Well, she had found a good story. I was soon engrossed in what appeared to be the tale of the famed white buffalo killed in 1876 on Deep Creek in what is today Scurry County, Texas. Like the Old Blue papers, the story was written in the first person. Though not altogether unheard-of in American literature, stories by animals were certainly rare. Robert Lawson, of course, found and published a few. Lawson's most famous volume was *Ben and Me*, about the mouse who helped Benjamin Franklin with many of his finest discoveries.

As with all manuscripts of this type, there were significant questions about the provenance of this "diary." There were few clues to answer them. The inner envelope had a postmark of 1917 from Lawton, Oklahoma. Both the pencil address and return address had been erased so thoroughly that the envelope was thin and discolored where they had once been written. The middle envelope had a December 21, 1971, postmark from Waco, Texas, but both the address label and the return label had been removed. The outer envelope, a padded mailer, was simply addressed to the West Texas Collection and had a 1986 postmark from Midland, Texas. A note in the same handwriting as on the envelope's address said: "Perhaps this will be of interest during the Texas Sesquicentennial celebration."

Whether the envelopes had any relation to the ledger's origin and author is uncertain. We can only speculate at this date so far removed from the creation of the diary itself. The Lawton, Oklahoma, postmark is certainly curious because of its proximity to Fort Sill. It was at Fort Sill that the Comanches surrendered their freedom and were introduced to the reservation. Life on the reservation ended their days on the Texas plains. In the text are many references to a young Comanche brave who took the name "White Buffalo." It may be that the story of the actual buffalo was told by this Comanche brave. He may have written it down or passed it on through the oral tradition of the Comanche, to be recorded later. Either way, it is written in pencil by a feeble hand. The Waco and Midland postmarks are equally inexplicable.

At this late date it is impossible to determine

whether this document is in any way authentic. It tells a poignant story about the last days of the buffalo and the fate that befell them. This is all seen through the eyes of the famed white buffalo. Perhaps it is an allegory for the demise of the Comanche people. Shortly after they disappeared from the Texas plains, so did the buffalo. While on the one hand the "diary" seems too implausible to be real, on the other hand it seems too reasonable to be contrived.

After expressing to Suzanne my interest in publishing the diary, we then met with her supervisor, Dr. Maurice Fortin, director of the Porter Henderson Library at Angelo State University. Dr. Fortin graciously granted permission for me to publish the book. I contacted Eakin Press, where the publisher and editors were as excited about the book as I was.

What follows, then, is the memoir as I transcribed and edited the text for publication. I cannot decide whether the account is true or not. My mind says it is impossible for the memoirs to be authentic. My heart, however, wants to believe that they are. I will leave it for the reader to make the final decision.

After all, it is the reader's opinion which is the most important of all.

—Preston Lewis
San Angelo, Texas

X

Chapter 1

❧ ★ ❧

What It's Like to be Different

Blanca is my name. I was different from all the buffalo that inhabited Texas. Unlike my kin and all the others that ever roamed Texas, I was born white.

Momma always said I was unique, but many buffalo called me a freak. As a result, life wasn't easy for me. I cried many a night because of what the others said about me. Their taunts burned my ears for many moons. But I grew accustomed to the teasing. I learned that it is your soul that makes you beautiful, not the color of your hide or your hair. It took me years to understand that, even though Momma told me so all along.

This is a story of what it is like to be different. Among the sea of dark brown hides, I always stood out. At first it bothered me. Later, though, I realized that the traits that made me different also gave me strength and brought me my greatest happiness. They brought me a mate who would father my children and watch over us and the herd. His name was Echo, and he grew up to be the biggest and most powerful bull buffalo I ever saw. This is his story as much as mine, because ultimately the whole herd owed its survival to Echo and his smarts.

I must start at the beginning, the occasion of my birth. Momma always said I was born under a Comanche moon. It was called a Comanche moon because it was so bright that under it you could see the Comanche Indians traveling at night. They rode their war trails south to steal horses from the white settlers. Momma said she had never seen a Comanche moon so bright as on the night I was born. It was bright enough to be daylight. The buttes and canyons and mesas of West Texas were awash in white light. Momma thought the moon's glow bleached my hair and left me white. That is as good an explanation as any.

Momma was so proud of me that she didn't really care that I was different. She loved me as I was. Her friends, though, were less understanding. They wanted her to call me "Snowball" or "Blizzard" or some ugly name like that. Momma told them that my name would be as pretty as I was. They must have snickered and tried to hide their giggles at Momma's foolishness. How could anyone find beauty in a freak like me?

Momma did.

"Her name," she announced to her friends, "will be Blanca. She will be remembered long after the rest of us are gone."

Surely the others laughed. They must have shook their heads and marched off to gossip among themselves about my ugliness.

I don't remember any of that, though. What I recall is finding myself on wobbly knees in the most beautiful world imaginable. It was spring, and the earth was covered with lush grass and flowers. The flowers were so bright it was as if a rainbow had crashed to earth and drenched them with its magnificent colors. The vivid carpet of grass and flowers extended to the mesas and buttes, which towered like great monuments against the dark blue sky. The mesas were layered with muted slivers of red, yellow, brown, and gray. Surely that was the ground where God had experimented with the hues He would ultimately put in the rainbow.

I thought I was the luckiest buffalo calf ever born. My world was so glorious. Nature seemed so wonderful. I didn't realize that some of the beautiful plants had thorns or barbs on them. They could hurt you if you were not careful.

Later I would learn that nothing could hurt you as much as your own kind.

Momma taught me about the seasons, about night and day, about the sun and the moon, and about the Comanche. Like us, they were nomads. They roamed the plains and badlands of Texas to find good water, lush grass, and a place to sleep. Their lives were intertwined with ours. They virtually worshipped us, but they sacrificed us, as well. In death we provided meat for their children, blankets for their elderly, clothes for their women, adornments for their men, and shelter for them all. Momma explained it as the cycle of nature. Everything had its time and its place. Certainly the buffalo had secured its place on the plains. Momma told me that millions of buffalo roamed Texas at the time of my birth. The Comanche numbered but in the thousands. That was how the world should have been. We could not foresee the world changing for the buffalo, but it would.

For me, everything was an adventure. I chased butterflies, stuck my nose down prairie dog holes, watched the hawks flying overhead, and waded in spring-fed streams. I was just learning how to be a buffalo. I didn't yet know that I looked different.

I did observe that the others tended to watch me a lot. I thought it was because I was beautiful.

One day when I was playing in a creek and splashing water, I glimpsed a strange-looking buffalo calf. I snapped my head around to see who had joined me. I was standing by myself. I looked around again. Had I had missed someone who had slipped up on me? No! No one stood in the creek but me. I stood motionless. As the waves of my splashing flattened out, I stared at the reflection. A white calf stared back. Slowly, I lowered my head. The white buffalo lowered its head, too. I blinked. The reflection blinked. I raised my foreleg. The reflection did, as well. I lifted my hoof out of the water, then lowered it again. The reflection did, too.

I was frightened. The reflection was me!

I bolted from the water and charged to the only one who had the answer to everything.

"Momma, Momma," I cried. "I'm white! I'm white!"

"You're special, Blanca, you're special."

"But Momma, I'm different from the others."

Momma smiled. "Of course you're not like the others. You're special."

I began to cry. "I don't want to be special."

"We are all different from each other, Blanca. It's the way of nature."

I looked around me. All the buffalo were brown. The color of their hides varied but slightly. Oh, how I wanted to be just like them. I sobbed. Momma nuzzled against me to comfort me.

"Blanca, if everything was the same, the world would be so drab," Momma explained.

Tears trickled from my eyes and fell to the ground. Though I bawled in front of the herd, Momma remained patient.

"Good comes from everything," she said. Her voice was as soothing as a cool breeze. "Even your tears bring good."

"How?" I mumbled through my tears. "They don't feel like it."

"Like a gentle sprinkle, your tears give moisture to Mother Earth."

Glancing down, I saw that a couple of tears had landed on the ground and another on a bluebonnet petal. The tears seemed too small to provide much moisture. Then a bumblebee buzzed by the flower. He circled a moment. He lit on the petal beside my teardrop. He seemed to drink my tear. Then he flew away. I should have felt better, but I didn't.

Momma spoke patiently. "Without differences, the world would be a boring place and Mother Earth a sad mother."

I wondered how Mother Earth could be sad. She was touched by the blue sky and sprinkled with colorful flowers. She was traversed by cool, refreshing rivers and was dotted with sculptured buttes, mesas, and canyons. I shook my head. I tried to stop my tears, but I was too sad not to cry. "I just want to be like the others," I managed between sobs.

"You want to be the same as them?" She shook her head toward a couple of playful calves.

I nodded meekly.

"But Blanca, do you think Mother Earth would want everything to be the same?"

I answered tentatively. "I guess."

Momma shook her head toward a colorful vista. The flowers seemed to sway in unison and wave at us. The buttes stood magnificently before us. "If the flowers were the same, there would be only one color and one shape. If the land was the same, it would be flat and monotonous. And the sky, if it were the same, would be cloudless. Without clouds, we would have no rains to quench Mother Earth's thirst. We would have no shade to shelter us from the burning sun on hot summer days. Blanca, though you may wish to be the same, you are too young to understand what that would mean."

I tried to grasp what Momma was saying, but my heart was heavy. I was sad and embarrassed. Maybe if I were just a little different, I could accept myself. Instead, I was always the first calf to be noticed in the herd. The others stared at me. That left me nervous and uncomfortable. I just wanted to live my life without everyone pointing me out. Most of all, I didn't want to be mocked.

"Blanca," Momma said, "you are unique, no matter what anybody else says. You'll make friends. They'll see you for the fine being that you are. But whatever they think, I'm proud of you. I always will be. I love you as only a momma can."

I snuggled against Momma's chest. It comforted me to know how much she loved me in spite of my blemish. I thought she was as beautiful as the flowers that carpeted the land in front of us. She had a graceful set of curved horns which were dark like her eyes. Those horns I stared at a lot. I couldn't wait to grow up and have horns like hers. I never did see a more beautiful buffalo than her. How someone as different and ugly as me could have been her daughter confused me.

Not only did I look funny, I also was a shy calf. Buffalo are a sociable lot, sticking together in great herds for companionship and fun.

The other calves my age had begun to play with each other. They romped over the prairie, chased rabbits, splashed each other in the creek, and made general mischief. I stayed close to Momma. I was afraid the others might make fun of me, or worse, just ignore me.

Momma recognized my shyness and decided it was

time to do something about it. "Why don't you go play with the others?" she implored.

"I don't know them."

"You never will if you don't play with them."

"They'll make fun of me."

"No more than they make fun of each other now. They laugh when one slips in the mud or steps in a prairie dog hole."

"They don't laugh at them because of their color. They'll laugh at me, you just watch."

Momma lowered her head and nudged me toward them. "Go tell them your name."

"I don't know them."

Momma began to nod toward each one and tell me their names. "There's Judy, who was born a couple days before you, and Teresa, who was born about high sun the day you arrived. There's Carla and Sandy—they were born shortly after you. That's the girls. And then the boys are Dobie, Prescott, and Battus. Watch out for those boys. Don't let them get you in trouble."

"I'm scared, Momma."

She pushed me harder.

"Ohhh!" I looked at her. There was granite in her eyes. She intended to force me to meet the other calves. I took a deep breath to bolster my courage. I ambled toward them.

I eyed them warily as I moved their direction. My heart wasn't in it.

They stopped their playing as I neared. Each one looked at me. The boys smiled. The girls were more suspicious.

Stopping a dozen paces from them, I swallowed hard. "I'm Blanca."

"We know," said Teresa, rolling her eyes.

Prescott strode over. "Why haven't you played with us before?"

Before I could answer, Teresa responded. "I think she's just stuck up."

Her words hurt me as much as any that were ever said. I wasn't stuck up. I was shy. I almost ran back to Momma. I felt my lip quiver like I was about to cry.

Then Battus spoke the prettiest words I ever heard.

"I-I-I think she's b-be-beautiful."

Chapter 2

Battus and an Important Discovery

I was touched by his words, but the others made fun of Battus. They taunted him for stuttering. They mocked him for calling me beautiful. Because he stammered, they called him "Echo."

I had feared they would make fun of me. Instead they were making fun of the one who complimented me. I offered a small smile of thanks to Battus. He winked at me. The others laughed at him.

"Echo likes Blanca! Echo likes Blanca!" Judy and Teresa called. Soon Carla and Sandy joined in.

Unlike me, Battus did not let their mockery bother him. He just smiled and walked among them. He took their ribbing without complaint. I admired his confidence. I wished I were as self-assured as he was.

When Prescott and Dobie took up Judy's taunts,

Battus lowered his head and charged the two. They laughed and scattered before he could butt them. After that, both quit chanting. Eventually, the girls got tired of mocking Battus. They went to play among themselves. Shortly, Prescott and Dobie found a rabbit to chase. Battus lingered nearby. When Battus and I were alone together, he became suddenly shy. He dipped his head and dug at the ground with his front hooves.

He offered me a timid, almost embarrassed grin. "M-m-my name is B-ba-battus."

"Thank you for calling me beautiful."

"I-i-it's true," he replied. "I-I-I can't even say my own name. B-ba-battus. S-se-see?"

"But you said nice things about me," I reminded him. "The others mocked me."

"T-th-they mock me, too. C-ca-call me 'Echo.' I c-ca-can say Echo clearly, b-bu-but not B-ba-battus."

"I will call you Battus."

He grinned shyly. "Y-y-you can call me Echo. I-it-it sounds nice when you say it."

"How do you stand their teasing? I wanted to run away when they said I was stuck up."

"T-th-they always b-ba-band together against someone who's different."

"That's not nice," I answered.

"B-bu-but that's life."

Echo was a realist. He saw things as they were and adapted. He was also smart and cute. I was pleased when he wanted to play.

"W-wh-why don't we go to the creek?" he said.

As we trotted toward the water, I glanced over my shoulder. I saw Momma smiling at me. She was pleased I had found a friend.

At the creek we played in the water, laughing and carrying on. When we tired of that, we bounded out of the water. We made up a game we called "buffalo herd." We kicked gravel from the creek bed and piled up the stones, like a great buffalo herd grazing. Echo found one stone that was as white as snow and he put it at the head of the herd.

He moved the rock with his nose. Then he looked up at me. "T-th-this is my favorite rock," he said, "b-be-because it reminds me of you."

I smiled and then found a black stone to represent him. I nudged it with the hoof until the rock was beside the white stone. "Now we can play together," I said.

"N-n-no," he replied, "we're leading a great herd."

Shortly, I noticed Judy and Teresa edging closer toward us. Our laugh-ter had sparked their curiosity. They marched up beside us and demanded to play. We told them to start their own herd of stones.

"No," Judy replied, "we want to play with yours."

Echo shook his head. "N-no-not after what you said about B-bla-blanca. S-sh-she's not stuck up."

Angrily, Judy marched through our herd of stones. She kicked and scattered them. Then she trampled into the soft ground the white stone and the black stone Echo and I had picked for each other.

"S-sh-she's not mean like you!" Echo shouted at Judy.

Judy lifted her head in the air as she spun about. She pranced by like she was the brownest and prettiest buffalo in the world. "Come on, Teresa, let's go. We've got better things to do." They and strutted away to join Carla and Sandy.

"Let's play herd again, Echo."

He shook his head. "W-wh-why don't we chase grasshoppers?" he offered.

"But what about the stones we selected for each other?" I saw them half buried in the soft ground where Judy had stomped them.

"L-le-let's mark the place so we can find them again when we want to play with them."

Echo dug up a larger stone with his hooves. He pushed it with his nose until it covered the two rocks we had been playing with. "T-th-this stone will mark the place whenever we return," he announced.

Then we scampered away, running over the prairie, chasing grasshoppers and laughing. We might have strayed too far had not Momma and Echo's father been watching us. They dampened our enthusiasm and made certain that we didn't run out of sight. Away from the herd, a wolf might attack us. Buffalo were so big and traveled in such large numbers that wolves and other predators could not threaten us unless a newborn calf wandered away.

While we were playing, Echo actually picked a bouquet of flowers with his teeth and laid them at my feet.

"Thank you."

His smile flattered me as much as the flowers. I wondered if my father had ever given Momma flowers. I would have to ask Momma. My father had been sacrificed by Comanches when they attacked our herd just before I was born. He had shielded Momma from attack. She had escaped with her life and with mine. I was born three weeks later.

By midday, Echo and I were tired and hungry. We wandered back to the herd and to our mommas for a meal and for a nap.

"Did you make some new friends?" Momma asked.

"One," I answered. "Battus."

"It's a shame he can't talk any better than he can," Momma replied.

"Don't say that, Momma. He's special. He wouldn't be Battus if he talked like you and me."

Momma smiled broadly at me.

I knew I had pleased Momma, but I didn't know why. "What is it, Momma?"

"You made my point, Blanca."

"What point?" I was confused.

"Battus wouldn't be Battus if he didn't stammer, you said."

I nodded.

"There's no difference between him and you, then."

I still failed to understand.

"Battus wouldn't be Battus if he didn't stammer. You wouldn't be you if you were any color but white."

Momma had made a point. She was wise. When I was young, she always tried to share her wisdom. I didn't always appreciate what she was trying to teach me, though. After all, as I grew, I thought I knew a lot more than I did.

Echo and I became great friends that summer. We explored the broken country beneath the Llano Estacado. We wandered with the herd between the Brazos and Colorado rivers. We always sought sweet

grass and cool water. We chased grasshoppers and rabbits. We watched fish swimming in the clear waters of
the creeks. We pestered prairie dogs. We ran races
across the prairie and watched the clouds pass like a
herd of fluffy white buffalo. Among those white clouds,
Echo would find one that reminded him of me. He always would flatter me and make me feel like I was the
prettiest buffalo in all of Texas.

Some days we would play with Judy, Teresa, Carla,
Sandy, Prescott, and Dobie. I was ever careful to address Echo as "Battus" in front of them. I never wanted
any of the others to think I was mocking him. Every
time we played together, Judy would always find some
way to insult the color of my hide. Teresa was just like
her, only she couldn't think of insults as quickly as Judy
could. Carla didn't like it that Echo treated me nicely.
She started telling others that he must be stupid, especially since he could barely talk. Sandy was always trying to get Prescott and Dobie or occasionally even Echo
to fight over her. She thought she was so pretty. Echo,
though, knew she was a phony. He stayed away from
her. Further, he didn't care if Carla thought he was stupid. The more time she spent insulting him, the less
time she spent gossiping about me.

I didn't like them as much as Echo, but both
Prescott and Dobie were fine boys. Though more bash-

ful around me than Echo was, they were decent and trustworthy. When I was busy with Momma, Echo spent time with Dobie and Prescott. I never saw Echo play with Judy, Teresa, Carla, or Sandy without me being around. That made me feel good, because I knew he liked me.

The spring of our births turned into summer. The grass and flowers began to wilt. The clouds thinned out. Though fewer, the clouds brought patches of precious shade from the hot sun. The creeks and rivers ran more shallow. Thunderstorms released more lightning and thunder than rains.

Echo was curious about everything, not just me. He listened to his father's recitation of the wisdom of the plains, passed down from generation to generation of buffalo. He remembered the locations of the springs which could be counted on for water during the driest summers. He learned to stay away from creek- and riverbeds after thunderstorms to avoid dangerous flash floods. Sometimes water rushed down streambeds so fast that a buffalo could not escape the gushing waters. He observed the direction that geese flew so he would know when a change in the weather or the seasons was approaching. He discovered what plants could be eaten and when they were tastiest. Just as importantly, he fig-ured out which plants could make you sick. And he learned how to defend the herd and how to lead the escape when Comanches approached. Besides that, he was so smart that he discovered things no buffalo who preceded him had ever understood.

I was with him when he made an amazing discovery: Buffalo have poor eyesight.

We had ventured from the herd farther than we should have. We picked up the scent of a coyote and heard the squawking of a bird to the west. Echo stopped and listened for a moment.

"L-le-let's see what the commotion is about, B-bl-blanca."

"I'm scared," I replied.

"I-I-I'll protect you," he assured me.

So, I accompanied him farther from the herd than I had ever been before. We eventually topped a rise and saw a mangy coyote at the base of a yucca plant. The coyote was laughing and carrying on beneath the yucca plant while a hawk circled nervously overhead.

As we neared the yucca plant, we saw that the coyote was toying with a small bird. The coyote swatted at it with his paw, occasionally glancing at the larger hawk flying overhead. In a small nest of twigs in the spiny leaves clumped at the base of the yucca stalk, two other infant birds watched wide-eyed. They squawked as the coyote threatened their sibling.

The coyote was hunkered beneath the yucca leaves so closely that mother hawk above could not swoop in and attack him with her talons. Further, the coyote was so focused on the baby hawk that he did not hear us until we were right behind him.

"H-how-howdy, Mr. Coyote," Echo said. "M-my name is B-ba-battus. W-wh-why don't you leave that little b-bi-bird alone?"

The coyote looked over his shoulder. He was bug-eyed and sneering when he saw us. Drool dripped from his yellowed teeth as he ran his purple tongue over them.

"I was hunting a snack, but it looks like I've got a whole meal here with you two young calves."

Suddenly, I felt scared. I wanted Momma, but Echo never trembled. "W-wh-why don't you leave that little b-bi-bird alone?" he insisted.

The coyote laughed. "Ca-ca-can't you talk, Battus, or whatever your name is?"

His mockery of Echo angered me. Echo stood firm, never blinking in the face of danger. During the conversation, the tiny hawk eased away from the coyote. The frightened bird never took his eyes off of those yellow teeth.

When the coyote reached for the bird, Echo lowered his head and butted him in the gut. The coyote yelped and tumbled from beneath the protection of the yucca spikes. Instantly, the mother hawk swooped down from the sky with talons bared. She clawed at the coyote's ears and neck.

"Ouchhhh!" he cried. He spun around and swung his paw at the ascending hawk. He backed up but ran his rump onto one of the sharp spines on the yucca plant. He jumped and yelped again. "Ouchhh!"

When he glanced at the yucca plant, Echo charged him a second time. Echo hit him under his front legs and flipped him. The coyote went tumbling end over end in a cloud of dust. As he was trying to stand up, the mother hawk attacked again. She slashed his neck and back with her talons.

The coyote screamed again. Unable to protect himself from both a ground and air attack, he scrambled away. As the coyote retreated toward the horizon, the hawk glided to the ground. She landed just inches from where her baby was crying.

"I've told you a dozen times, you're too young to fly, Elroy. You must listen to your mother." She picked him up with her beak. She flapped her wings and leaped to the nest amid the yucca leaves that protected her young from predators. Dropping off her disobedient son, she lifted her wings and jumped toward us. She landed on the ground in front of Echo.

"My name's Lamy," the hawk announced. "I'm grateful for you saving my boy. I couldn't get close enough to the coyote with him hiding under the yucca plant.

"I-I-I'm Echo," he announced. "M-m-my friend is B-bl-blanca."

"Thank you both," Lamy said. "Elroy wants to fly before it's time."

"C-coy-coyote shouldn't b-bo-bother you again. H-he's prob-ably all the way to the Canadian River by now."

"Oh, no," answered Lamy. "He's over there in a clump of prickly pear."

Both Echo and I looked, but we didn't see any-thing.

Then Lamy pointed with her wing. Still, we did not see the coyote.

Though I didn't want to admit it, I didn't even see the clump of prickly pear she was pointing at.

Echo was not so embarrassed. "Wh-wha-what prickly pear?"

"I don't see it, either," I whispered to Echo.

Lamy spread her wings and hopped on Echo's

back. "I'll show you." She turned to her nest. "Elroy, if I come back and you're not in that nest, you'll get no supper."

"Yes, ma'am," he replied.

Then Lamy pointed us to the clump of prickly pear and rode Echo in that direction. I followed. We were halfway there before Echo and I made out the clump of cactus. We could just barely make out Coyote running away into the distance.

"Did you see him escaping?" Lamy asked.

"Yes," I answered, while Echo just nodded.

We went all the way to the prickly pear and touched it just to prove the plant wasn't a mirage.

As we returned to Lamy's nest, Echo shook his head. "M-my-my, we can't see very well."

"Must be all the hair from your hide blocking your vision," Lamy said.

When we reached Lamy's nest, I became frightened. Sunset was approaching and I couldn't see the herd. The wind was blowing from us toward the herd, so there was no way we could pick up the scent, either. I was afraid we were lost for good.

Lamy hopped off Echo's shoulder. Elroy and his siblings were calling for supper.

"Can I return a favor for you saving Elroy?" Lamy asked.

Echo nodded. "W-wo-would you take to the air and find our herd? W-w-we need to rejoin them, but we can't see them."

"Sure," Lamy responded. "And better yet, I'll keep an eye out for Comanches while you are in the vicinity."

"W-we-we'd be obliged to you if you would."

Lamy raised her wings, then lunged into the air. Her powerful limbs took her skyward quickly. Within a minute, she was pointing the way back to the herd. Echo and I trotted in that direction.

"Thank you again," Lamy called after us.

Chapter 3

The Legacy of Magnus, and a Birthday Celebration

Summer gave way to fall. Then fall gave way to winter. With each day, the earth cooled. The grasses that had wilted under the summer heat began to yellow and die. Our coats began to thicken for the winter months ahead. All the time we young buffalo were growing and maturing physically.

Echo and I stayed closer to the herd after the reprimand from our parents. We gradually lost some of our childhood curiosity. We began to understand the world around us and the way of the buffalo. We moved south to find ungrazed land and to escape the brunt of the winter at the foot of the Llano Estacado. The young ones like Echo and me learned to forage for food in the cold. We figured out how to dig out grass from under the occasional snow. The herd moved south all the way to the Concho River. With the approach of spring, we began to retrace our path north. The days lengthened, and the chill softened in the air.

By spring we had returned to the land of my birth. I loved this land of buttes, mesas, canyons, draws, and wildflowers. Then one evening at dusk, Momma came to me and gazed toward the east, where a giant full moon had arisen. It cast an orange glow in the twilight.

"That moon is special," she told me.

"Why?"

"It reminds me of the night you were born. When the sun disappears, the moon will glow white hot. The land will look like a ghostly day."

Momma and I watched the moon rise in the sky. The moon cast a peculiar glow that blanketed the land as far as I could see. It was a soft white light, not harsh enough to be day, but too bright to be night. Occasionally, I glanced from the moon to my white fur. I wondered if the moon had indeed bleached the brown from my hair.

Once I glanced at Momma and saw her eyes glistening with tears. "What's the matter?"

She smiled softly at me. "I was thinking how a Comanche moon like this brought such joy to me with your birth."

As I moved closer to comfort her, she began to cry. "What else is wrong, Momma?"

"I wish your father had lived to see you. He was a great buffalo. I had admired him from the time we were both kids. I enjoyed playing with him just as you do with Echo."

"Do you think he would have liked me?" I asked.

"Oh, yes, Blanca. He would have loved you."

"Even with my white fur?"

"Yes, Blanca. He died to protect me and you, still unborn inside me."

"What happened, Momma?"

"The Comanches came one morning. They rode against the wind so we could not smell their approach. We did not see them until they were right upon us."

When she said that, I realized how important Echo's discovery about our poor eyesight had been.

"We stampeded," Momma continued. "I ran as fast as I could, but I was heavy with you. I could barely trot, much less run. A pair of Comanches on horseback galloped up to me. They drew their bows and aimed their arrows at me. Your father saw my plight and charged to help me. He rammed the horse nearest me, knocking the rider to the ground. Then he darted between me and the second Comanche. Your father took the arrow that was meant for me. The arrow buried itself between his ribs. Your father stumbled, then staggered. The Comanche celebrated his aim, but your father would protect me until I got away. Your father charged into the horse. He downed both rider and mount. Then your father yelled at me, 'Run, mother-to-be, run! Save yourself and our unborn!' Those were the last words of your father. He had died, but the Comanches called off their chase. Instead, they tended the riders he had downed. Because of your father, all in the herd survived except him."

Momma cried softly. "Some say he still protects the herd. That the Comanches call us a ghost herd to be avoided because of his bravery."

"What was his name, Momma?"

"He was called 'Magnus.' His name is still respected by everyone."

"T-tha-that's true," came a voice behind me. Echo walked up to my side.

"Good evening, Battus," Momma said.

Echo nodded respectfully. "Y-yo-you can call me 'Echo,' like Bl-bla-blanca. I-I-I didn't mean to overhear you."

Momma smiled at Echo, then at me. "You've been such a good friend of Blanca's that I do not mind what you hear, Echo."

Echo smiled bashfully. "F-fa-father always speaks highly of Magnus."

Those words made me proud of my father. I wished I had had a chance to know him.

"I-I-I wanted to see if I could take Blanca for a walk? T-th-there's something I want to show her," Echo announced.

I was nodding at Momma, hoping she would say yes.

"You may, but don't go as far away as you did when you saved the baby hawk."

Echo nodded. "Y-ye-yes, ma'am. C-co-come along, B-bla-blanca."

I jumped to my feet.

"B-b-be quick, B-bla-blanca."

With that, Echo bolted away from Momma. I chased after him.

"What is it?" I called.

"Y-yo-you'll see."

Saying nothing more, he ran toward a low mesa. Then he bolted up a narrow trail to the top.

Curious, I followed. "What is it?"

He didn't answer. I didn't query him again, as the trail was narrow and treacherous. I was glad for the light of the Comanche moon. Otherwise, I might have stumbled along the rocky trail. When we reached the top of the mesa, I had an eerie feeling. Were we really alone? I scanned the mesa top but saw nothing unusual.

Then I heard the swish of wings. A familiar friend landed at our feet. It was Lamy. The hawk must have been the presence that I felt.

"Why did you bring me up here, Echo?"

"T-to-to show you something."

"What?"

"C-co-comanches," he announced.

I was scared. No wonder I had felt an eerie presence.

Echo led me to the far edge of the mesa. He shook his head to the north. On a trail below, a dozen Comanches rode single file along the foot of the mesa where we stood. They were magnificent, muscled men astride their ponies. They wore feathers in their braided hair. The moccasins on their feet and the breechcloths around their waists were made from buffalo leather. The thought chilled me. They carried long lances or bows and arrows. Their laughter drifted up to us.

Suddenly, I was terrified. These were the men who had killed my father and threatened my momma. "Are they coming for buffalo?" I asked.

"No," Lamy answered. "They are a war party, going south to steal horses from the settlers."

"Settlers? Who are they?" I had never heard of anyone by that name.

Lamy answered. "Settlers are people who stick to one plot of ground. They don't wander around like no-mads as the Comanches and even you buffalo do. They build giant, square wooden nests on the ground. Some even make their nests in the side of an embankment, living like ground squirrels."

These were curious beings, these settlers, I thought. "What do they do when they eat up all the food on their land? Don't they move then?"

"No, no," Lamy answered. "They plant seeds in the ground and grow food. Then they store it."

"But why do they do this when the earth provides so much?"

"They store the food to feed their children during the lean winter months. Even buffalo must keep moving during those months to find food."

"Strange people, these settlers," I said.

"W-we-we will not see settlers in these parts, surely," Echo said. "B-bla-blanca, I want you to remember what the Comanches look like. If you ever see any, you can escape."

We watched until the Comanches disappeared from sight, at least Echo's sight and mine. All the time I had the feeling there was another presence atop the mesa. I never could explain it. I was glad when we said good-bye to Lamy. We retreated down the side of the mesa. Once we reached level ground, Echo moved beside me. We returned to the herd.

"T-tha-thank you for coming with me, B-bla-blanca."

"Thank you for inviting me, Echo," I answered, "but one thing's bothering me."

"D-di-did I do something wrong?"

"No, Echo, of course not. How did you see the Comanches far enough away to get me in time to climb the mesa and see them before they were out of sight? Your eyes are not that much better than mine."

Echo grinned mischievously. "L-la-lamy said she would help keep a watch out for Comanches as long as we are around her. S-sh-she'll help protect the herd by letting us know of any nearby threats."

"That's kind of her."

"S-sh-she thinks she owes it to you and especially me for saving Elroy from Coyote last year. G-gi-give a kind deed and you will get a kind deed in return. T-tha-that's why you should help others. E-ev-even your father must have believed that."

"But he is not around for others' kindness."

"T-tru-true, but the others are kind to you and your mother."

"Judy, Teresa, and their friends are not kind to me."

"B-bu-but they're not grown yet."

"We're all growing up fast."

Echo didn't say a thing for a while, not until we neared the herd. Neither did I. I just enjoyed being close to him.

As we approached the herd, he stopped. He looked at me oddly.

I halted and turned to study his face.

"H-ha-has anybody asked you to the gathering tomorrow?" he asked.

"What gathering?"

"J-ju-judy and the others are having a get-together. W-we-we were all born this time of year around a Comanche moon. I-it-it's a birthday celebration. W-we-we won't be kids much longer. This is a chance for us all to have some fun."

"Are you going?"

"I-if-if you go."

"I haven't been invited."

"W-with-without you going, I won't go."

"But Judy and them don't want me around."

"S-su-sure they do, B-bla-blanca. T-th-they just haven't gotten around to asking you. T-th-they will tomorrow. J-jus-just wait and see."

"How can you be so sure?"

"D-do-dobie and Prescott told the girls they wouldn't go unless I went. I-I-I told them I wouldn't go unless you were invited."

As we neared the herd, I moved closer to Echo. I gave him a kiss on the neck. He seemed both pleased and embarrassed.

"T-th-the gathering is set for high sun. J-ju-judy will let everyone know where we will meet. W-we-we don't want our parents finding out and stopping us."

Echo saw me back to Momma's side, then went to join his parents. I had trouble sleeping. I couldn't decide if it was because of the odd light of the Comanche moon or because I feared that the other girls didn't care for me.

After I awoke the next day, Judy sauntered over. She was all prissy and proud of herself. She motioned for me to move away from Momma. I tried to sneak off without being obvious. Only after we were both away from Momma did Judy speak.

"You're invited to a gathering we're planning at high sun."

She didn't sound like she wanted me to come. Echo did, and that was all that mattered to me. "Are you sure?"

"Absolutely, Blanca," said Judy.

I could tell her words were insincere.

"We want everyone there, and we can't get everyone there without you."

I didn't care about being around her, but I wanted to be with Echo. "Okay, I'll be there."

She nodded toward the mesa that Echo and I had climbed the previous evening. "We'll meet on the opposite side of that butte. That way we can have fun without our folks seeing."

"I'll see you there at high sun," I replied.

"Sure you will, Blanca." Judy scampered away.

I returned to Momma, and a bit later Echo came running over.

"D-di-did Judy invite you to the gathering?" he whispered.

I nodded, fearful Momma might overhear.

"Y-yo-you're still going?"

I smiled and nodded again.

"Gr-grea-great," he answered. "I-I-I'll see you there."

Because Echo was happy, I was happy. I didn't care to be with Judy or her friends. At least with Echo around, I could tolerate them.

He scampered off. He called over his shoulder that he would see me there. He tripped as he spoke. I snickered as he disappeared into the herd.

About an hour before high sun, I walked to the creek. I took my fill of water. Then I started walking leisurely away from the herd. I hoped no one would see me escaping with the others behind the mesa. I made a wide loop away from the herd. Then I swung back toward the butte so I would not be spotted. It was a beautiful day. The sky was a pure blue. The land was a sea of waving spring grass and beautiful flowers. With so spec-tacular a sky and earth, I could not hide my happiness. Maybe the others would want me to play with them.

Just before high sun, I was the first to arrive. I waited in the shade for the others. I tried to forget how the other girls had treated me in the past. As I waited for them, I practiced smiling. I wanted to hide my sus-picions.

When high sun arrived, I was still the only one who had made it to the mesa. I knew Echo would arrive shortly.

I waited.

No one came.

Surely Echo would arrive.

Still no one came.

Had there been a mistake? Had I misunderstood? Surely not.

I walked to the far end of the mesa. There I viewed the herd. I did not see them among the others. Nor did I see any of them walking in my direction.

I felt my eyes flooding with tears.

Maybe none of them liked me, not even Echo.

Why hadn't anyone come? Did they still think I was a freak? Were they afraid to be seen with me? How could I ever face any of them again? Why had Echo abandoned me? It was a cruel trick. I began to sob.

I felt so embarrassed and helpless. I walked aimlessly around the mesa. When I found myself at the foot of the trail to the top, I marched up it. Some moments, I no longer cared whether I might trip and fall over the edge.

Atop the mesa, I moved away from the trail and the rim so no one could see me. I stood there lonely and betrayed. I sobbed uncontrollably. I vowed to stay there forever.

Somehow, through my hurt and my sobs, I heard the grunt of some animal, or so I thought.

I spun about. What was it? My heart quickened and my crying stopped. I was not alone. It was not an animal. It was worse than another animal.

There, not twenty paces away, stood a Comanche. Wild-eyed, he staggered toward me. He reached for me with outstretched arms.

I feared I was about to die like my father—at the hands of the Comanche!

Chapter 4

White Buffalo's Vision

The young Comanche staggered toward me. His wide eyes stared beyond the horizon. His hair was as wild as his eyes, as if the wind had been his comb. His lips were swollen and cracked.

As he drew nearer, my fear gave way to curiosity. He seemed too ill to be a threat, and he carried no weapon. He was too big to be a boy, but too young to be a man. He stumbled closer. He tried to lift his hand but was too weak to hold it up. As frail as he was, I knew he could never hurt me. He didn't have the strength.

Coming within reach of me, he extended his arm. It quivered. I stiffened, wondering if I should let this young Comanche touch me. After all, his kind had killed my father. Perhaps his own father had sacrificed my father. Even so, he was hurting. I felt sorry for him.

Odd as it seemed, I felt he needed me. His hand came closer. I raised my head to await his touch.

Just as he was about to touch me, I heard a squawk overhead. Glancing up, I glimpsed Lamy circling above us. She then flew away toward the buffalo herd.

As Lamy departed, the Indian half stepped, half lunged toward me. His hand grabbed at my forehead. His fingers tightened around my white hair. He leaned against me and put his arm over my head to support himself. His grip slowly melted away like snow before the sun.

"Ghost buffalo from the ghost herd," he whispered. He fell to his knees, then collapsed on his stomach. His breath seeped from his body. He was so still, I feared he was dead. I lowered my head and pushed him over onto his back. He moaned. I placed my nostrils against his nose and forced my breath into him. The touch of his skin was hot and fevered. Sick as he was, I knew that he needed water. He was too weak to walk to the creek. I could never get him to water. I did not know what to do. All I knew was that I could not leave him to die.

Overhead, I noticed buzzards circling and waiting for him to pass away. I could not let them touch him, but I could not save him without help. If I left, the buzzards might pester him until he died. He could not defend himself.

I was confused and overwhelmed with emotion. I had never felt so bewildered. I had been misled by Judy about the location of the gathering. I had been abandoned by Echo, my one true friend. I had to protect this young Comanche. He was as near a friend as I had. After all, he had never hurt me. I did not know what I was going to do, though. I felt so helpless.

For a moment, I imagined I heard Echo calling.

"B-bla-blanca."

How could I think of Echo now, when he had abandoned me for Judy and the others? The call came again.

"B-bla-blanca."

It was not my imagination. It was Echo. He barreled up the trail, bounced over the rim, and bounded toward me. He saw the Comanche at my feet.

"G-ge-get b-ba-back!" he cried. "G-ge-get b-ba-back from that Comanche!"

He dashed beside me and shoved me hard. He knocked my breath away, and I could not talk for a moment.

"D-di-did he hurt you?"

I shook my head and gasped, "No."

Echo glared at the helpless youth. Had the Comanche been a threat to me, Echo would have defended me. When he realized that the Comanche was unconscious, he looked at me. He dropped his head. He looked hurt. Silently, he just shrugged.

I felt sorry for him, but I had a question I needed answered. "Why didn't you and the others come?"

He looked bewildered. "I-I-I waited for you with the others at the creek."

"Judy told me to meet on the north side of this mesa. I was here before high sun, just like she said."

Echo raised his head. Rage flashed in his eyes. "S-sh-she told me she had invited you. S-sh-she lied to us b-bo-both, you the wrong location. I-I-I'm f-fu-fu-fur-fur-furio..."

"Furious," I said, finishing his thought.

He nodded. "M-my st-stut-stutter g-ge-gets w-wo-worse w-whe-when I-I-I'm m-ma-mad."

"How did you find me, Echo?"

"L-Lam-Lamy," he answered. "W-wh-when you didn't show up, I-I-I spotted her and asked her to look for you."

"But how did she find me?"

Now Echo grinned. "B-bla-blanca, of all the buffalo in West Texas, you are the easiest to spot. W-whe-when Lamy told me you were up here with a Comanche, I-I-I ran as fast as I could to protect you."

"Thank you."

He smiled and stepped toward me. "Ma-may-maybe we should return to the herd."

"What about him?"

"Le-lea-leave him."

"But I can't, Echo. He's defenseless, like Elroy was."

"E-el-elroy was a baby hawk. H-haw-hawks aren't our enemies like Comanches."

"But saving Elroy made Lamy our friend. She keeps watch over our herd, warning us of dangers we can't see. She even found me for you today. If we help him, perhaps he will help us someday. Maybe he will be a better friend than Judy."

"J-ju-judy's no friend at all."

Echo turned away from me and approached the motionless Comanche. Echo stood over the youth, shaking his head.

I eased beside Echo. "What is he doing up here alone, away from his people?"

"M-my-my father says that before a Comanche youth can become a man, he must find his medicine, his power. M-ma-many times, my father says, he has come across solitary bo-bo-boys on the prairie seeking their medicine."

Echo explained that the Comanche believed that the power of a boy's manhood was revealed to him in a vision that came during a solitary quest. The youth would leave his village a boy and return a man, if he received his vision. The vision was the most sacred event in the Comanche male's life. When he left the village, the youth would carry with him a blanket for bedding, a bone pipe, tobacco, and a flint and steel to make a fire. Dressed only in moccasins and a breechcloth and carrying but a pouch to hold his talisman, he would walk to a solitary place like the top of a mesa or hill. There he would not eat or drink until his vision came. After receiving his vision, the youth would interpret it and chart the future course of his life. Usually, the youth would take a new name.

As Echo explained the medicine quest, he looked around. Not twenty paces away, we spotted the blanket and the pipe, the tobacco, and the flint and steel. Echo walked over, grabbed a corner of the blanket with his teeth, and pulled it away. The grass beneath it was bent and yellow. "H-he-he's been here several days, four or more, from the look of the grass," Echo said.

Perhaps the Comanche's presence might explain the eerie feeling I had atop the mesa when we saw the war party on the move. He had made no fire except in his pipe. He had eaten nothing. He had drunk nothing. He must surely be dying of thirst.

Returning to the unconscious Comanche, I leaned over him. I breathed in his nostrils again. Then I began to lick his face.

"M-may-maybe we should just leave him." Echo was nervous about my intentions.

"No," I answered. "He is some mother's son. If I ever have an offspring, I would want someone to care for my calf when it was in need."

Echo didn't question me again. He recognized that arguing against my maternal instincts would be foolish.

Shortly, the Comanche youth moved. His eyelids fluttered and then parted. I could see his eyes through tiny slits. He reached up and stroked my chin. He spoke in a raspy whisper.

"Mother of all buffalo, as long as you live, so shall your kind. And as long as I roam free, then shall you roam free."

Echo looked at me. "I-is-is he delirious?"

I shrugged. I did not know. I did know I was not the mother of all buffalo.

Then the Comanche whispered again. "From this day forward, I shall be known as 'White Buffalo.'"

Echo looked at me. "I-i-it's an omen."

I doubted that, but Echo seemed convinced.

"E-eve-even if it's not an omen, I do not want to take a chance," he said.

"Take a chance on what, Echo?"

"H-he-he said as long as he roamed free, you will roam free, B-bla-blanca. H-he-he's even calling himself

'White Buffalo.' W-we-we must find him water so he will live."

Suddenly, Echo was concerned about the Comanche. He feared that the Comanche's future and mine were now linked.

"H-hel-help me get him up," Echo ordered.

We got behind him and pushed his shoulders with our noses until he was in a sitting position. Then we shoved our heads and necks under his arms. We pressed him between us and were able to lift him to his feet. Slowly, we started moving him toward the path down the mesa's face. At times he seemed to revive and walk with us. At other times he was almost dead weight. The trail was narrow, but somehow we squeezed together tightly enough to manage. We made it to the foot of the mesa without injury, though several times rocks gave way under Echo's feet.

I thought how foolish Echo had become. To make certain that I might survive an omen, Echo was willing to risk his own life.

My shoulders began to ache from the load, but I didn't complain. Echo was doing this for me, for my future. He was strong and smart. Like the youth between us, he was on the verge of becoming a man. I rejoiced that of all the buffalo I knew, he was my best friend.

After what seemed like forever, we reached the

creek. Echo and I were grateful that dusk was approaching. We did not want our parents to see us. They might not have appreciated what we were doing.

At the water's edge, we pushed the youth into the shallow creek. He splashed, then sputtered in the water. He took great gulps, then gasped for air. He crawled on hands and knees to the edge of the creek. There, he collapsed and rested. He let the coolness of the water bathe his burning skin.

As we backed away, I tripped over a rock and almost fell down. Echo jumped to my side, then looked at my feet.

"Re-rem-remember that rock?" he asked.

I shook my head.

"S-sur-sure you do."

I looked again.

"La-las-last spring we used gravel to pretend we led a buffalo herd. Re-rem-remember we b-bu-buried the stones here to represent us?"

"Now I remember," I said. "A black stone and a white one."

Echo shoved the rock away with his head and then dug the two stones free with his hoof.

As he did, the Comanche youth rose from the water. He stepped to us. He was still sluggish, both of foot and mind. At our feet he bent over, then picked up the two stones we had been talking about. He retreated to the creek and washed them off. Next, he held them to the horizon, where the sun was a dwindling ball of orange flame.

"Oh, young bull buffalo," he said to Echo, "this black stone I shall carry with me to symbolize the strength that brought me to water." He next turned to me. "Oh, mother of all buffalo, this white stone shall represent you and the future of the buffalo. Together you will be stone buffalo that I carry in my pouch to protect you as you have protected me."

He reached first to touch Echo, then me. He spoke to each of us as his fingers rubbed our foreheads.

"Oh, young bull buffalo, may you be the biggest and smartest buffalo of all. May your children be many and your wisdom great. But you must always beware of the horned toad, for he talks much and is not your friend."

Then he spoke to me. "Oh, mother of all buffalo, may you be fruitful upon the plains. May your children and your children's children and their children for many moons to come run across the plains. But, mother of all buffalo, you should fear the horned toad, for he is not your friend."

"Whenever I see you or you see me, we shall not fear one another, but you must be wary of the horned toad."

He said nothing more, but just put the two "stone buffalo" in his pouch. He retreated to the river. There he fell to his hands and knees and drank water like a buffalo.

When he finally stood, he said nothing as he walked past us toward the mesa to retrieve his things.

We watched him in the fading light. When we could no longer see him, we jumped in the creek to wash his smell from us. Only then could we approach the herd without alarming anyone.

"What do you think he meant about the horned toad?" I asked Echo.

"I-I-I don't know, but one day I will find out."

It had been a day filled with hurt and anger because of Judy's lies and betrayal. It had been a day of disappointment that Echo and I might doubt one another. And it had been a day of mystery about the Comanche and the horned toad.

But it was one of the most important days of our lives. We would see White Buffalo many times over the coming years. He and his warning would help us protect our herd and each other.

Chapter 5

~★~

Becoming a Young Woman

I accompanied Echo the next day when he found Judy and her friends. Echo was so angry he could barely talk.

"W-wh-why d-di-did you lie to B-bla-blanca?" he shouted.

Judy sidled over to me with a big grin on her face. "Lie to Blanca, the white freak? Why would I do that?"

"T-ta-take that b-ba-back," Echo demanded.

Smugly, Judy lifted her nose in the air. "It's true. She's a white freak, but I never lied to her. I told her we'd gather at the creek, just like I told everyone else."

Echo took a step toward Judy. He was shaking with anger. "I-I-I di-did-didn't say what the lie was about. Y-yo-you seemed to know enough anyway to cover it up with another lie."

"B-bla-blanca could be lying," Judy mocked Echo.

Her mockery infuriated me. I lowered my head and charged into her ribs. I knocked her to the ground. Then I began to kick at her as she tried to get up.

Teresa, Carla, and Sandy rushed me. I was so mad I spun around and stared them down. Seeing my rage, they realized it was unwise and unsafe to challenge me. Judy, though, jumped up and ran into my flank. Pain jolted through me for a moment. I spun about and lowered my head to meet her next charge. Our heads butted, and we both staggered back for a moment. We pawed at the ground, then began to circle each other.

Before we could attack again, Dobie and Prescott raced up. They got between us and pushed Judy away while Echo ran to me.

"S-sh-she shouldn't have called you a name, B-bla-blanca," he stammered.

"I don't care what she calls me," I said as I began to cry. "I didn't like her making fun of you."

"Th-tha-thank you, B-bla-blanca, but it doesn't b-bo-bother me. S-sh-she can't stammer as well as I can, anyway."

I couldn't help but laugh.

Echo just grinned. "L-le-let's get away from them."

Judy was talking about how mean and ugly I was. Teresa, Carla, and Sandy were joining right in, calling me names and calling Echo stupid and dumb.

Prescott and Dobie tried to calm them down. Both liked Echo, but when they were around the girls, they didn't correct them.

Echo and I hiked to the creek. We kicked stones into the water and laughed at the splashes. Then we crossed the creek and wandered among the wildflowers. Echo picked some with his mouth and laid them at my feet. I was proud that he thought well of me.

I began to dream of life with Echo. I knew what a fine buffalo he would be and what a fine father he would be for our offspring.

"Wh-wha-what are you thinking?" he asked me.

"About the future," I replied.

"I-I-I've been thinking, too."

I moved closer to him, hoping he had been thinking of life with me, too. I felt he thought as much of me as I did of him. "What have you been thinking about?"

"T-th-the Comanche and what he said. 'B-be-beware the horned toad.' I-I-I don't understand."

I was disappointed that Echo hadn't been thinking about me. Even so, our future seemed to depend upon heeding the warning of White Buffalo in his vision quest.

"T-tha-that's been bothering me all night and day, m-mo-more than even Judy's meanness."

"How can horned toads threaten us?"

"I-I-I don't know. M-ma-maybe we need to find a horned toad to ask."

We spent the rest of the afternoon searching out horned toads. They were squat little creatures, not long and sleek like most lizards. Instead, they had a rough back with little spikes atop it. Two little horns crowned their heads. We found a couple dozen scurrying about, hiding beneath plants and rocks.

"Hi, little friend," I would say. I tried to make their acquaintance, but most ran off. Of course, we could have chased them and caught them. However, if they didn't want to talk to us, we couldn't force them to. We just wanted to understand why we couldn't trust horned toads. It was hard to see any horned toad as a threat to the buffalo. They were tiny compared to us, and we were just yearlings. By the time we were full-grown, we would be massive by comparison.

Echo decided to let me do the talking if we found one that would answer our questions. It was midafternoon before we came upon a talkative toad. He was a big one we found napping in the shade of a patch of bluebonnets. He was fat and lazy. When he awoke, he eyed us, then spat at our hooves.

"Afternoon, little friend," I said. "How are you today?"

"Fine until you interrupted my nap," he answered.

"We're sorry. Let me introduce us. I'm Blanca and he's Battus."

"If you're really sorry, why don't you just wander on? I'll get a little more sleep."

"We've a few questions."

"We, girlie? Sounds like you're the only one that's got questions. Doesn't your boyfriend there have a tongue?"

"Y-ye-yes, I do," Echo said.

The horned toad laughed. "Sounds like you've got two tongues in your mouth."

I didn't like the little reptile's mockery. I had to fight the temptation to step on his tail.

"What have you got against the buffalo?"

"For one, they interrupt my nap."

"We're sorry."

"For two, you trample the ground and destroy our homes."

"We don't mean to," I replied.

"Then you kill us by the hundreds."

"What!" I shouted. "I've never killed a horned toad and don't intend to."

He spat again at my hooves. "You know what it's like to be in a stampede? Thousands of black hooves churning up the ground all around us. It's like thunder in the earth. Every stampede, you kill hundreds of us. You say you don't mean to? There's millions of you. There's no escaping you. I dream about the day there will be more of us than of you. I'll do anything to see that day come."

"That's not a very nice thing to say," I responded.

"It's true, though." With that, the horned toad turned around and waddled away.

I was upset by his harsh words, but Echo wasn't. Now he knew what the Comanche meant and why horned toads despised the buffalo.

"T-th-the horned toad must tell the Comanche where we graze. W-we-we've learned much today, B-bla-blanca."

Together we walked quietly back to the herd.

Momma was awaiting me. "Hello, Battus, I would like to talk to Blanca alone."

"Y-ye-yes, ma'am," he said.

I knew I was about to be scolded for my fight with Judy. So did Echo.

"B-bla-blanca fought after Judy mocked me," he said. "I-I-I just thought you should know that."

"Thank you, Battus. Now be on your way." Then Momma fixed her eyes on me. "Blanca," she said, "you are getting too old to be fighting with others. You are no longer a kid."

"But she made fun of Echo, Momma. She stuttered like he does."

"That's not what her mother says. Judy's mother said you called Judy vile names, then attacked her."

"It's not true, Momma. Judy's a liar."

"Don't call anyone a liar."

"But what if they are lying, Momma? What if they are lying? What should I call them then?" I began to cry. Judy had lied to me and to her mother. Now my momma believed Judy's mother.

"It's not ladylike to call someone else a liar, Blanca."

I felt so helpless. To defend my actions, I had to tell the truth. The truth was that Judy had lied to me and to her mother. "She lied to me about the gathering place. I went to the mesa, like she said, but nobody came. She lied so I wouldn't be able to play with the others. And today, she called me a 'white freak.' I ignored her mean words until she made fun of Echo. That's when I attacked. Echo's my only friend, Momma. No one else likes me."

"Don't call Judy a liar."

"But Momma," I cried back, "haven't you taught me to tell the truth always?"

"Yes, Blanca, but you don't call others a liar."

I stamped my hooves on the ground because I was so frustrated. Judy had told several untruths. That was the truth. That made her a liar. I stood there shaking in frustration.

Momma stepped beside me. "I know you are upset, Blanca. Except for Echo, I know the others don't always treat you nicely. I know it's because of your looks. Maybe they don't want to be seen with you. Maybe they don't like you."

"Judy doesn't," I huffed. "She's always trying to humiliate me."

"All of you are going through a difficult time in your lives. You're changing from youths into young adults. There are emotions you must learn to deal with. Soon, all of you will begin to grow horns. When that happens, you will be young adults. You'll start pairing off as mates, like Magnus and me. Then you will have your own offspring to raise and to help through their early years."

"I hope they're not white."

"Blanca, that's a horrible thing to say."

"It's true," I replied.

"You're special, Blanca. You were born that way for a reason."

"Whatever the reason, I don't like it."

"It won't matter what you think as long as your mate likes you—and one will."

"I hope it's Echo. He understands me."

Momma smiled. "He's a nice one. And, if it's not him, it will be someone else."

"I hope it's him."

"Just promise me one thing," she said.

"What?"

"When someone's lying, don't call them a liar. It's such a vile word."

"But what if they are lying? Isn't it truthful to say so?"

"Blanca, maybe it is truthful, but it's not mannerly. I want you to be mannerly."

"Yes, ma'am."

With that, Momma sent me back out to play. "Enjoy your youth while you can," she called out to me.

Soon spring turned to summer and summer turned to fall. Mostly I played with Echo. Sometimes I joined in with the others. I always felt like an outsider among them. Whenever they chose sides, I was always the last one picked.

Gradually, we lost interest in the games we had played as kids. In the fall, Judy became the first to grow horns. They emerged as little nubs on her head. She was so proud, acting as if she was grown. She treated the rest of us as if we were still kids.

Next Echo began to show horns, then Dobie, Sandy, Carla, and Teresa. For several weeks only Prescott and I lacked horns. Each morning when I woke up, I would run to the creek. I would wait for enough light to see my reflection. Most mornings, I left disappointed, particularly the day Prescott strutted by with nubs of horns.

Judy and Teresa teased me about still being a kid as their horns grew longer and blacker. I worried that my horns would be white. It would be yet another reason for everyone to dislike me or make fun of me.

Once Judy, Teresa, Carla, and Sandy grew horns, the boys paid more attention to them. Even young bulls who were a few years older began to hang around, wanting to court them.

I wondered if any of the other young bulls might want to court me once I grew horns, or if it would just be Echo. After Echo had begun to grow his own horns, he started to look at me differently. I couldn't explain why. He was a bit more awkward around me. For once, he seemed to be embarrassed of his stutter around me—me the white buffalo.

One morning, I looked at my reflection in the creek and saw a couple of nubs poking out of my head. It was a proud moment for me. I looked once, shook my head, and studied the water again. Yes, I was going to have horns. I was going to be a young woman, who would be courting before long.

I marched back to Momma and showed her my discovery. She complimented me on how nice I looked. I was proud. But much as I loved Momma, I really wanted to hear what Echo thought. I was dying to know if he still thought I was pretty. He had called me beautiful when we were kids. I wanted to know if he still thought so.

Wandering away from Momma, I found Echo lounging in the grass with Prescott, Dobie, and some older bulls.

Dobie greeted me first. "Hi, Blanca, you're looking mighty fine today."

Since he had grown his horns, Dobie had become quite the charmer. He complimented every young female, regardless of his interest in her.

"Morning," Prescott said. "My, do I see a set of horns beginning there?"

I nodded. I turned coyly around to face Echo.

He smiled. "M-mor-morning, B-bla-blanca." Then he turned back to the others.

I was confused—why didn't he say more to me? When Prescott and Dobie started talking to the guys, I walked away. I hoped Echo would follow me.

When he didn't, I was very disappointed. I strolled

across the prairie and accidentally came upon Judy, Teresa, Carla, and Sandy. They were resting near the creek after bathing. They gossiped about all the young bulls. They didn't notice me as I neared. Or if they did, they just ignored me.

"Dobie's got such a way with words," Teresa said.

"So has Echo," Judy responded, and all the girls laughed.

I cleared my throat, then walked among them. "Good morning," I said. Much as I disliked them, I wanted them to see the nubs of my horns.

Carla was the first to notice. "Well, well," she said, "look who's becoming a woman."

"A pale woman," Judy just had to say.

I ignored her and settled on the grass with them. I listened to their conversation. I knew they weren't interested in what I might be thinking.

Sandy and Judy argued over which one of the two was prettier. They tallied the number of young bulls that had escorted them on moonlight strolls.

"The secret to attracting a young bull," Judy announced, "is to be unpredictable. You must make them jealous. Nothing works better. Find one you like, show him your charms, then go after another bull. That makes him want you all the more."

"It helps to be pretty," Sandy said, batting her eyes at me.

I was uncertain whether she was complimenting herself or insulting me.

"Yes," Teresa said, "pick out your beau, but don't let him think you're too interested. You've got to play hard to get."

I listened to them gossip for a spell, but not one of them was interested enough in me to care what I had to say. I slowly rose and walked away. They were just as glad that I was leaving.

When I reached Momma, I wanted to know what she thought about boys.

"What did everyone think of your horns?" Momma asked.

"Prescott mentioned them. Echo didn't say a thing. Then I visited with the girls. Judy was insulting, as always. Though Carla did notice my horns, nobody else said much about them. Mostly, I wanted Echo to notice, but he didn't say a thing to me. Before he grew horns, he would talk to me all the time."

Momma looked thoughtful for a moment. "Lie down and let's visit," she said.

When we were both comfortable in the grass, Momma spoke. "Boys and girls are different. You know that."

I nodded.

"When you're young, those differences don't seem that major. When you become a young adult, things change. You recognize those differences for the first time. It can make things awkward. You see each other not just as play friends but also as life mates. Some try to hide the awkwardness they feel by being the center of everything, like Judy, or by trying to act more mature than they are, like Dobie."

"But, Momma, Echo seems more shy than ever before. It's like he doesn't want to talk to me."

"It's not that, Blanca. It's just that he doesn't know the right thing to say. His father was as shy a young bull as I ever saw. Battus probably takes after his father. I think you and Battus will become life partners, but it may take time. Just be patient, Blanca. Just be patient."

Chapter 6

The Future of All Buffalo

Despite Momma's advice, I was not patient. At times I pestered Echo, trying to get an indication that he still liked me. We were growing. We were no longer kids, but we weren't full-grown. My horns developed. They were a shiny black that contrasted with my white fur.

Echo's horns developed, as well. His body became bigger and stronger. He changed in many ways. He didn't talk as much. I was uncertain if he had grown more embarrassed with his stammering as he matured or if he was just going through that awkward stage like me. He wasn't a loner. He got along well with the other young bulls, but he was shy around me and the other young females.

He never forgave Judy for lying to me, but he was never rude about it. He didn't care that Judy, Teresa,

Carla, and Sandy thought him dumb. Sometimes he seemed distant, as if he were brooding over something. Was it me? I did not know. I didn't think so, but I wasn't sure. Was it something else? Perhaps, but what? The only female he talked to regularly besides me was Lamy. Perhaps it was Lamy that worried him so. It was almost as if he thought the survival of our herd, of all buffalo, depended on him.

Sometimes when the herd would move, Echo would range far ahead of the others, weaving from side to side along our path. The others thought he was crazy or had been out in the hot sun too long. Even though he never told me, I had an idea he was warning the horned toads of our approach so they would not be trampled as we passed. I never told anyone my suspicions. Had I told someone, they would have laughed at him. After all, how could a little horned toad threaten animals as majestic as the buffalo? As long as Echo ranged ahead of us on the move, we never once were bothered by Comanches. Because of him, the horned toads had no reason to betray us.

As we wintered near the Concho River, Echo would sometimes wander away from the herd. I never knew where he went, or why. Maybe, like the Comanche named White Buffalo, he had to find his power. Maybe it was just because he was a thinker. I think he was respected by the elders of the herd, but at times they probably underestimated him because of his stammer. He thought more and worried more about us than I suspect any buffalo ever had.

After one of his journeys, I was waiting for him as I always did during his absences. I would stand a vigil each night, hoping that he would return. I wished that he would show as much interest in me as he had when we were kids. I never lost faith in him, however. When I saw him approaching, I ran away from the herd to greet him. He was especially worried. His brow was furrowed, his lips were tight, and his eyes were nervous. He seemed to have aged more than his years.

"Welcome back," I said.

He smiled weakly. "B-bla-blanca, how nice of you to come out to greet me."

I smiled back. "You are the only one that will talk to me."

"I-I-I know b-be-better than that. B-bla-blanca, you are the only one who doesn't mock my speech. T-th-the young bulls tolerate me b-be-because I am as b-bi-big as them, b-bu-but you've always been the one who accepted me as I was, never doubting me."

"And you have always accepted me?"

He grinned. "B-bec-because you were always so pretty. Y-you're still pretty, with your white fur and your b-bl-black horns. Th-ther-there never was a prettier young buffalo than you, B-bla-blanca."

Those were the words I had waited to hear. I nuzzled up against his neck and kissed him. He tried to smile but did not return my affection.

"What's the matter?" I felt sad that he seemed to be so depressed. When he hesitated to answer, I feared that he had found someone else in a herd far away, someone he liked more than me. "Is there someone else?"

"Y-ye-yes," he answered.

My heart failed me for an instant, until he continued.

"Ma-man-many," he said.

I didn't understand.

"Se-set-settlers," he said. "And ahead of them, the men who wear b-bl-blue coats and carry guns and fight the Comanche."

"Where are these people?"

He pointed to the Concho. "O-on-on this very river they built a huge nest they call a 'fort.' Th-the-there are many b-bl-bluecoats. As many as in a bed of ants."

"But if they fight the Comanche, won't the Comanche save us?"

Echo pondered for a long time before answering. "I-I-I don't know. T-th-the settlers behind them dig up the grass and b-bu-build fences to keep others out.

W-we-we cannot live on a land like that. I-if-if they come closer, we cannot survive as we have. T-th-the Comanche depend upon us for survival. If the Comanche are driven from this land, who's to say that we, too, won't be driven away?"

"But there is so much land, Echo."

"Th-ther-there's only *so much* land, B-bla-blanca," he replied. "O-on-only the sky is limitless."

We walked back to the herd without another word. All the males welcomed him back. Most of the females greeted him as well, save for Judy, Teresa, Carla, and Sandy. They were too busy flirting with all the other young bulls to care about Echo like I did.

As winter gave way to spring, we headed north again. We grazed our way back to the foot of the Llano Estacado and the land where Lamy still flew. Echo always walked ahead of us, warning the horned toads so they would not tell the Comanche where we were.

Then one day, the whole herd had a great scare. We caught the scent of Comanche! That was unusual in itself because Comanche usually came from downwind so we would not pick up their scent. They turned out to be a raiding party headed to the land of the settlers, but they came close enough for us to see them. As they neared, Echo planted himself between them and the herd.

The riders drew nearer, and I saw them draw their bows and arrows. I feared for Echo and broke from the milling herd. I trotted to him. All but one of the Comanche pointed to me. He alone rode toward us. As I stopped by Echo's shoulder, I recognized White Buffalo. Then I heard his voice drift over the land to us.

"Mother of all buffalo, as long as I live and roam the prairie free, so shall you live and roam the prairie free."

His voice was strong, unlike the raspy whisper I remembered when Echo and I had first encountered him.

With that, he raised his lance over his head and let out a whoop that increased the nervousness of those behind us. Then he and the other Comanches turned their war ponies to the southeast and rode away.

When they rode out of sight, Echo nodded to me. "B-bla-blanca, you were right," he said. "W-we-we helped save that Comanche, and now he has helped save us."

When the Comanches were gone, several buffalo came to congratulate Echo on driving them away. "B-bla-blanca deserves the credit," he said. "S-sh-she saved the life of the young Comanche who called to us."

"Yeah," said Judy, who had just walked up. "Blanca's such a freak, she frightened them away."

Her remarks made Echo so furious he could barely speak.

"J-ju-judy, y-you-you're s-so m-me-mean."

By his stuttering response to Judy, I knew Echo still cared for me.

We gradually made our way back to the land of my birth. It was good to again see high mesas and buttes. The rains came frequently that spring. The land was carpeted with as many flowers as I had ever seen. They were so pretty, they made me sentimental. I wanted so badly for Echo to court me. I wanted to be his mate for life. But Echo was not as anxious as I was to court. I was hurt.

And then one morning before sunup, he came to me and nudged me from my slumber. "C-co-come with me, B-bla-blanca," he whispered.

Blurry-eyed, I arose while Momma still slept. I followed Echo. He trotted away from the herd toward the mesa where I had found White Buffalo when he was seeking his medicine.

"What is it?"

"L-la-lamy says someone wants to see us."

"But why must we run away from the herd?"

"W-whi-white Buffalo."

"The Comanche?"

Echo nodded.

We went up the trail that we had last traversed while getting the youth down to the creek. The many spring rains had eroded gaps in the trail, so we had to be careful as we climbed. We reached the top just as the sun was breaking across the eastern horizon. The low sun cast a blood red light across the broken land. Behind the buttes lay dark shadows that reminded me of giant buffalo carcasses stretching all the way to the horizon. As I topped the rim, I saw White Buffalo seated before a small fire in the middle of the plateau. He smoked his medicine pipe.

Echo and I approached the fire. We stood downwind so the smoke would blow over us and disguise the scent of the Comanche. Otherwise, the herd might be alarmed when we returned.

"Oh, mother of all buffalo, you have returned."

I nodded.

"And the great young bull."

Echo dipped his head in acknowledgement.

"I knew you would come. I saw it in my dreams. You are powerful medicine. You are the future of your herd, the future of all buffalo," White Buffalo said. Then he began to chant and to strike a small drum that sat before him. When he stopped, he looked at Echo. "You have questions?"

Echo nodded, then, with his hoof, drew in the dirt a crude representation of a horned toad.

White Buffalo studied Echo's drawing. "The horned toad is not your friend," he said.

Echo knew that.

"The horned toad is not your friend. Whenever the Comanche ask a horned toad where the buffalo are, the horned toad will run in the direction of the nearest herd. A horned toad pointed our war party to you when we passed a moon ago. The horned toad cannot be trusted."

Echo shuddered, his sudden movement startling me. I knew he was not scared. It was just his way of communicating with the Comanche warrior.

"You ask why I should be trusted?"

Echo nodded.

"When I came upon your herd with the war party, I saw the mother of all buffalo with you. We rode away without harming you. Did we not?"

Again Echo nodded.

"The mother of all buffalo will save the herd from death. I have seen it so many times in my dreams. The mother of all buffalo has the heart of her father, a brave buffalo. As long as I roam the prairie, the mother of all buffalo will be safe. As long as she is brave, the buffalo shall be safe."

I didn't feel brave. I felt confused. Why were all of

these responsibilities falling upon me? I was just a young female wanting to spend the rest of my life with Echo. I could not carry the fate of all buffalo upon my shoulders.

White Buffalo seemed to sense my doubts.

"Oh, mother of all buffalo, we are all born to our fates. You were chosen for this. You cannot stop your destiny any more than you can change the color of the sky. Because of you, the buffalo will survive. Without you, the buffalo will all die. I have seen it in my visions. You have given me powerful medicine."

From his waist he lifted a pouch and held it before our noses. He lifted the flap and pulled out two stones, a white one and a black one. They were the stones we had given him the previous spring at the creek.

"These stones carry your power. They give me true visions of the future. You will protect your own and save the herd. It is told by the Great Spirit. Do not deny your destiny, nor will I deny mine."

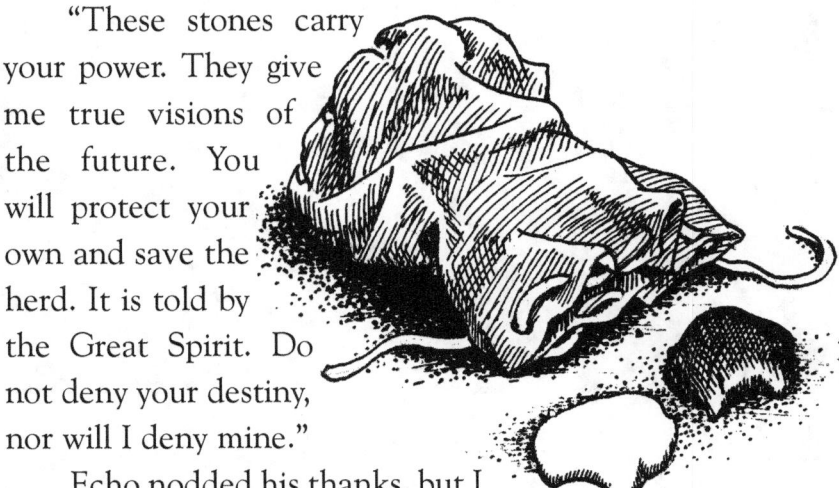

Echo nodded his thanks, but I

was too confused to acknowledge his words. We backed away from White Buffalo and retreated to the trail down the mesa.

"It is scary, what he said," I told Echo.

"B-bu-but you must accept that you are special, not just to me, but to all b-bu-buffalo."

I smiled. Those were the words I kept wanting to hear from him again and again. I knew that one day he would be my mate for life. What I didn't know was that soon my impatience would drive him away.

Chapter 7

⚬—⭐—⚬

Dobie Comes a-Calling

The rains continued to come that spring, giant thunderheads building to the west and dumping rain upon the land. Never had I seen the flowers so beautiful. The grass was sweet and so thick that we didn't have to roam to find plentiful food. The creeks ran during the entire summer. The Comanches did not bother us, just as White Buffalo had promised. It was a pleasant time, when the world seemed at peace with the buffalo.

I was not at peace with myself, because I realized I was in love with Echo. The more distant he had become, the more I felt drawn toward him. Echo was always courteous and respectful, but he didn't flirt with me. Now that we understood the differences between us, we did not know how to act around each other. There seemed to be a barrier between us that hadn't been there when we were innocent children. I thought Echo still liked me. Even so, he seemed as if his mind was always on something other than me. My mind, though, constantly held thoughts of him.

None of the other young bulls showed any interest in me, but that didn't matter. I was only interested in Echo. I always felt awkward with the young bulls, unlike Judy and her friends. They would flirt with one, lead him on, and then drop him for another. Somehow that kept them in the minds of all the young bulls. Several of Judy's suitors would follow her around, laughing with her and her friends. There always seemed to be a contest between Judy and Sandy to see who would have the most young bulls trailing them about.

Dobie and Prescott had been led on by both of them, then dropped for older bulls. I felt sorry for them and wished they could see what phonies Judy and Sandy were. They never did. Certainly Judy and Sandy were fine-looking. Certainly they were more beautiful than me. Their beauty, though, did not extend all the way to their souls. They manipulated their suitors. Even so, the young bulls fawned over them and made them think they were the most enchanting creatures on earth. Teresa and Carla attracted their share of young males, as well. Though they didn't draw as many as Sandy and Judy, they drew more than I did. I attracted no one, save Echo, and at times I was not certain about him. I couldn't tell if he truly liked me enough to be the mother of his children. Perhaps he was just too kind to break the ties that had bound us during our childhood.

Echo never followed any of the other young females around until one late afternoon. A giant thunderstorm, dark and menacing, loomed to the west. The aroma of rain drifted heavily across the land. The entire herd was nervous, except for Judy and her friends. They were laughing and carrying on as if they didn't have a worry in the world. Perhaps they didn't, with as many beaus as they attracted. Perhaps I was the only one that ever worried about the future and about finding a mate.

Sandy convinced Judy, Teresa, and Carla that they should go down to the creek and bathe. They all thought it was a great idea, seeing as how everyone else was so jumpy. So, they sauntered off to the bend in the creek where the waters had gouged out a bluff deep enough for them to hide behind and bathe. I, of course, was not invited.

After they wandered off, I saw Echo ambling toward the bend in the creek. I didn't think anything about it at the time. I just thought he had gone there to watch the storm. I could see him profiled against the dark sky. He

was a handsome young bull. I enjoyed just staring at him. I wondered if he ever enjoyed looking at me.

Then something happened that changed our lives. Judy and Sandy appeared from behind the bluff, still wet from their baths. They were mad and bellowing. I didn't understand what the problem was until the two accosted Echo.

"How dare you spy on us while we are bathing!" Judy yelled.

"Have you no honor?" Sandy shouted. "We have our modesty."

By then, Teresa and Carla had joined Judy and Sandy.

"Oh, this is so embarrassing," Carla said.

"Do you think we'd be interested in some one as stupid as you?" Teresa cried. "Well, think again, Echo. There's nothing about you we like."

"You stay away from us," Judy cried, shaking her head at Echo.

With that, all four females turned about and marched indignantly back to the herd. They made a point of informing everyone they encountered about Echo peeping on them.

Poor Echo! He stood so forlornly by himself. He seemed an outcast. Part of me felt sorry for him. I am ashamed to admit that a larger part of me was mad at him. There he was, looking at other young females while they bathed. He had barely looked at me recently. I was hurt.

He was so embarrassed, as well he should have been. He did not return to the herd until darkness had enveloped the land. The huge cloud seemed to have snuffed out the sun. I might never have seen Echo's return had not lightning bolts streaked across the sky. Nearly everyone was nervous, milling about.

Echo was embarrassed when I walked up. I was still mad. Further, I was humiliated. The one young bull that I thought liked me was peeking at other females I didn't care for.

"What were you doing over there, Echo?" I demanded.

"W-wat-watching for ..." he stammered.

"I could tell you were watching. Who is it you're interested in? Is it Judy? Don't tell me it's Judy. What about Sandy? Or is it Teresa or Carla?"

"N-no-none of them, B-bla-blanca."

"And I thought you liked me."

"I-I-I do, B-bla-blanca."

"Then why were you spying on them?"

"I-I-I was watching the clouds, B-bla-blanca, and the rain."

"Sure you were, Echo." I spun about and ran away.

I felt betrayed by the only young bull that had ever shown an interest in me.

Finally, I cried as hard as I remembered ever crying. No one realized it, though, because the clouds opened up and dumped rain on us. I wanted to run away, not as much from the cloud as from the embarrassment. Echo had taken an interest in Judy or one of her friends.

The herd stood its ground that night, though we were sopping wet come morning. My spirits were down. It amused me only slightly that Judy and her friends, in spite of their baths, were mud-splattered and dirty like the rest of us.

The rain had been so great that the creek had flooded during the night. The morning clouds were gray, matching my mood. I was still hurt from Echo's betrayal. I was also fearful of losing him. He stayed away from me that day, so I had a lot of time to think. As much as I disliked Judy and her friends, I had to admit that they had had more experience dealing with the young bulls than I had. Maybe they were right! Maybe making a young bull jealous was the only way to win his heart. Oh, how I wanted to keep Echo for myself.

About midafternoon, I summoned my courage and approached Teresa. She scowled at me. "What do you want? Why aren't you with Echo? None of us is interested in him, not with his lack of manners."

"He said he was watching the clouds and the rain."

"Ha," Teresa shot back. "He was snooping on us, trying to spy on us as we bathed. None of us appreciated that, not from someone as stupid as him."

"Echo's one of the smartest buffalo that's ever lived."

She laughed. "Is it true he's announces to the horned toads that the herd is approaching? That's what I've heard. It just proves he's crazy."

"I still like him."

"You can have him." She turned to walk away to Judy.

"I like him, but I can't tell if he's interested in me."

Teresa stopped and turned around. "Well," she said, "you are white, aren't you? I don't know that anyone else would be interested in you."

Her words stung, but I would endure anything to attract Echo.

"I was hoping you might help me win him."

"What?"

"I was hoping you might help me win Echo."

"How?"

"By making him jealous."

Teresa smiled broadly, then glanced toward her friends. When she looked back at me, she nodded vigorously. "We'd love to help you win Echo, because none of us want him. You stay here."

With that, she turned about and strode over to Judy, Sandy, and Carla. They listened to Teresa, then giggled among themselves. Together they all four came over.

"We'd be glad to help," Judy announced with a big smile. "Just give us until tomorrow to decide how to go about it. We'll make sure Echo will get his due. Just promise us one thing. Don't say a thing to Echo until we return to you."

"Okay."

They marched off, giggling and laughing. I felt a little uneasy having shared my feelings with them, but I was getting desperate. I had to win Echo, or I feared there would forever be a void in my life.

The night was a long one. I could not sleep. I didn't know what Judy and her friends would come up with. I was ready to try anything so that Echo would look at me only. I wanted him to spend the rest of his life with me.

Dawn finally came, and then the morning. Still no word from Judy and her friends. High sun passed, and they did not come. I did see Echo wandering about on the perimeter of the herd. He was too humiliated to join the rest of us. Once, I saw Teresa out visiting with Echo. I wondered why, but they only visited for a few minutes. Then Teresa rejoined the herd.

When night came I was depressed, wondering if it had all been a mistake. I slept poorly again the next night and was relieved when Teresa and Judy walked over. They were smiling.

"It's all set," Judy announced.

"Hard as it was to convince him to be seen with you, Dobie has agreed to come calling on you," Teresa said.

I didn't understand why Teresa had to be so insulting. She hurt me by stating things the way she did. I would swallow my pride if that's what it took to gain Echo's love. "Teresa," I asked, "what were you talking with Echo about yesterday when I saw you two together?"

"I, ah, we, ah . . ." she stammered.

"She told him," Judy interjected, "that we were sorry we had accused him of watching us bathe. We knew he was only watching the clouds."

"Yeah," Teresa said quickly, "that's what we, er, I told him."

"This afternoon," Judy informed me, "Dobie will come a-calling. He will escort you around the herd so that Echo will see you. Just pretend you are enjoying your time with Dobie."

"Dobie'll be pretending, too," Teresa said.

"Okay," I replied.

"We'll be watching," Judy said.

They walked away chuckling. I had never seen them laugh so much as over the last two days.

As they walked away, Momma came over. She looked at Judy and Teresa, then at me. "What's going on, Blanca?"

I was too ashamed to admit how I had been plotting with Judy and Teresa. "Oh, nothing," I answered.

"It's terrible how they treated Echo the day of the big rain. He's not one to do something like that. There's not a deceitful bone in his body."

"I know, Momma, that's why I like him." I wondered if Momma knew I was planning to deceive Echo just to make him jealous.

"You treat him nicely and I know things will work out for you. The two of you are made for each other." Momma turned and went on her way.

For the first time, I noticed the limp in her walk, and as I looked at her I realized she was getting old. I felt sorry for her, but not as sorry as I felt for myself. Otherwise, why would I be going through this deception with Judy and Teresa?

Come afternoon, Dobie found me, according to plan.

"Care to join me for a stroll, Miss Blanca?" he announced.

"Indeed I would." I smiled, and the two of us began to walk among the herd. We took our time, making sure we were seen by everyone.

Dobie was a good talker. He was smooth in all he said. Every word came out flawlessly. He never stuttered or stammered. He was so unlike Echo. And yet being around Dobie made me care for Echo even more. Dobie was a good young bull. He liked to be with others and was comfortable with them. By contrast, Echo was a little bit awkward and uncomfortable.

Out of the corner of my eye, I happened to glance at Echo. I could see the hurt on his face. If that was the look of jealousy, it made me sad. His head drooped. He turned away from me. I didn't want it to be painful for Echo. I just wanted him to pay more attention to me.

Later, as we strolled around, we came close enough to Echo for him to hear us.

"Would you care to go for a stroll tonight in the moonlight?"

"I would be delighted," I answered, then snuggled closer to Dobie. I could not bear to look at Echo. His pained expression would have been like an arrow in my heart. I thought jealousy would make him run to me. Instead, he seemed to shrink away. It was not working like I hoped.

Dobie left me for a while, then returned after sundown, and we went to watch the moon. It was a full Comanche moon. I saw Echo standing apart from the herd in the distance. Alone, he just stared at us. I knew he must have been feeling the pain that I had felt when he was spying on Judy and her friends. This was what I had intended, but I didn't know it would hurt me so much to do this to him.

"Oh, Dobie, I feel so bad, pulling this trick on Echo. I want him to like me so."

"Why, Blanca, don't worry about that. He likes you very much."

"But he never says so to me."

Dobie grimaced.

"What's the matter, Dobie?"

"Well, it's supposed to be a surprise."

"What is, Dobie?"

"Well, I've been helping Echo with his speech. He wants to stop his stuttering before he asks you to be his partner. You're the only one he's ever cared about. Fact is, a lot of us fellows think you're cute, but we know Echo's always been partial to you. We didn't want to hurt him."

My mind was awhirl with confusion. I leaned over and kissed Dobie. "Thank you, thank you. Echo can talk the way he talks. I don't care. I love him like he is. I must find him and let him know."

"He's a proud young bull, though, and may want to show himself that he can talk without stuttering."

"You care for Echo, too."

"I do," Dobie replied. "He's sincere and as smart an animal as ever was born into this herd."

"If you like him so, why did you agree to be seen with me like this?"

"Teresa and Judy told me that it would make Carla jealous if I was seen with you. I sort of like her. They said Echo didn't mind you and me being seen together. You think I should have asked Echo?"

"Maybe. I don't know," I answered hurriedly. "Thank you, thank you," I cried, "for letting me know how he feels about me. Now I've got to go find him before I hurt him even more."

I raced away charging through the herd, almost causing a stampede. Even under a Comanche moon I could not find him.

Echo had abandoned the herd. And me!

Chapter 8

❈

Where's Echo?

I cried all night, hoping Echo would return the next morning. He did not. I told Momma how I had tried to make Echo jealous, and the result. She said little. She didn't have to. I realized how foolish—how wrong—I had been to play with Echo's emotions. I had played the same games that Judy and her friends had. I was as mean as them. On top of that, I had hurt the best friend I ever had. Besides, I had been a liar. I may not have told an outright lie like Judy had, but I had lived a lie for a few hours. I wondered how many days I would have to live without Echo.

Dobie came by the next morning.

"Has Echo returned?" I asked.

"No," he said, hardly hiding his anger.

I began to cry because I felt Dobie was mad at me. Further, I did not know if Echo would ever return. "I'm sorry. I'm so sorry. I wish Echo were here so I could tell him myself. It's all my fault."

"No, it's not," Dobie said. "We were deceived. Last night after I left you, Blanca, I overheard Teresa and Judy bragging to Carla and Sandy about how they had tricked us."

"Why?"

"They never liked you because you were different. You remember seeing Teresa with Echo?"

I nodded.

"Well, she was telling Echo that you liked me instead of him. That hurt his feelings." Dobie bit his lip as it began to tremble.

I thought Dobie was about to break down like me. What he said next made me sob.

"Echo began to cry when Teresa told him you liked me more than him," Dobie said. He gritted his teeth for a moment. When he spoke again, his words were hard as granite. "When she told the others about him crying, they all laughed, every one of them, Judy, Teresa, Carla, and Sandy."

By then I was bawling. I had hurt beyond my full

understanding the one friend that had meant more to me than any other I had ever known.

"I'm sorry, Blanca. Echo was trying so hard to speak without stammering. He wanted to ask you to become the mother of his children."

If only I had been more patient. If only I had not turned to Teresa and Judy. If only I hadn't been jealous when Echo had spied on them bathing. There were so many things I wished I could have changed, but I could alter not a one, not then, not ever.

"He'll be back," Dobie said, trying to ease my concern. "He cares too much for you not to return."

"I don't think so, Dobie. If he believes you and I are courting, he won't ever come back."

"We should wait a few days and see. If he doesn't return, I'll search for him. Until then, if there's anything I can do for you, please let me know."

"There's nothing, Dobie, but thank you anyway."

He smiled gently. "One thing I will do for you is promise never to associate with Teresa, Judy, even Carla. They are a curse upon our herd." Dobie walked away.

Standing nearby, Momma had heard everything Dobie and I had said. "Liars, Judy, Teresa, all of them."

I was shocked by Momma's anger and her choice of words. I also thought it was Momma's way of apologizing for disciplining me when I had called Judy a liar.

I moped about camp for two days, hoping that Echo would come back, but he didn't. On the dawn of the third day after he left, I was awakened by the shrill call of a hawk. Opening my eyes, I looked skyward and saw Lamy. She signaled for me to meet her by the creek. I ran to the bluff over the watercourse's bend, where Echo had stood the night I had accused him of snooping on Judy and her friends.

Lamy landed at my feet. "I have message for you."

"From Echo?"

She nodded. "He said that he wished you and Dobie much happiness and many offspring."

"But I don't care for Dobie."

"He said he saw you kiss Dobie."

"I did, but only after Dobie told me he was working with Echo to lose his stutter before he asked me to become his partner. I was so excited that Echo was doing that for me that I kissed Dobie as I would a friend."

Lamy shook her head. "That's not how Echo saw it."

"I know, I know."

"He even says one of the young females told him you liked Dobie more than him."

"She lied," I said.

Lamy walked around me. "That is serious. Lying about such matters is a grave sin that violates the honesty of nature. No good can come from such lies for those who spread them." She eyed me suspiciously. "I hope you are not lying to me now."

"No, Lamy, I promise. I am trying to make up for the terrible deception I played on Echo."

She nodded. "I believe you."

"Would you do something for me, Lamy? Would you go find Echo and bring him back?"

"I don't know that I can do that, Blanca."

"Why not?"

"He made me promise I would watch out over the herd as long as you were in it. He cares deeply for you."

Tears clouded my eyes. I had hurt him, and even then all he thought about was my safety and security. "Surely you could find him."

Lamy sighed. "What to do? He has a two-day lead, long enough to be with another herd."

"But Lamy, you can find him."

"Blanca, you don't understand. Save for you, all buffalo look alike from the air. I could find you, but you are not lost. Echo looks like all the rest."

"Please. Echo's the one who saved Elroy."

Lamy pondered my plea. "I will ask Elroy to watch over the herd in my place. He is young but trustworthy. I will fly for two days and two nights. Then I will return."

"Thank you, Lamy, thank you."

"I'm sorry for you, Blanca." Lamy lifted gracefully from the ground and flew away. Later I saw a young hawk circling overhead keeping watch over the herd. I knew it was Elroy.

Word of the trick that Judy and Teresa had played on Echo and me spread among the herd. Dobie told Prescott, Prescott mentioned it to his friends. The whole herd was disgusted with Judy, Teresa, Carla, and Sandy. Their foolishness was no longer cute. Even the young bulls shunned them. For the first time, I realized how much the others in the herd had respected Echo. Certainly he did not speak perfectly, but he was smart and honest. I missed him deeply.

Dobie still felt guilty for his role in Echo's departure. He visited me every day to see if I had heard anything from Lamy or Echo. No word came on the first day, the second day, or the third day. Then about midafternoon on the fourth day, I noticed two hawks circling above.

Lamy had returned!

I darted away from the herd. My hopes were high until Lamy swooped out of the sky and landed a couple paces from me. I could tell by the sadness in her eyes that she had failed.

Lamy shook her head. "I saw many buffalo herds, but I did not find him. Perhaps he was among them. I cannot say, for I could not have asked each one."

"Thank you, Lamy, and thank Elroy."

"I will," she said. "And good luck to you."

No sooner had she flown away than Dobie dashed up. He read the sadness in my eyes, but asked the question anyway. "Any word on Echo?"

"Lamy couldn't find him."

Dobie sighed. "I've got to go after him, Blanca."

"But he has a six-day lead. No telling where he might be by now, Dobie."

"I've talked it over with Prescott. He'll go with me. "Echo's too good and too smart a bull to lose to another herd. I want to set things right."

To show my thanks, I walked over and kissed Dobie on the cheek. I had kissed him twice. That was as much as I had ever kissed Echo.

Dobie walked away. Within a few minutes, he and Prescott left the herd and marched to the southeast in search of Echo. To the northwest, a giant cloud was building and blocking the sun. Oddly, though, a hole broke through the clouds and a shaft of strong light shone on Dobie and Prescott as they walked away. I took it as a good omen. Shortly, the two young bulls had disappeared from sight and the shaft of sunlight evaporated.

In the distance, the storm clouds began to roil and roar. Bright daggers of lightning flashed within the clouds, to be followed moments later by great bellows of thunder. Despondent over Echo's absence, I stood and watched the clouds for an hour or more. I remembered how when we were kids Echo would always find a cloud that reminded him of me. That was a pleasant memory. Then I recalled the recent evening when Echo had stood at the crook in the creek while Judy and her friends bathed.

The thundercloud reminded me of all the bad things that had happened after the previous thunderstorm. Nothing, though, bothered Teresa, Judy, Carla, and Sandy. They decided it was time for another creek bath. I think they were trying to show the herd that they didn't care what any of the rest of them thought. They were going to continue to do whatever they pleased.

As they walked by, Teresa called out, "Th-the-there's B-bl-blanca. Wh-whe-where's E-e-echo?" Her friends just giggled as they slipped down the embankment into the creek.

I was too hurt by their cruelty to say anything. I just stood there aching for Echo. The giant thunderhead drew closer. The cloud flashed with a brilliant light. Thunder boomed and shook the earth. The cloud was dangerous. The herd huddled together to await the rain, but it never came. The cloud had loosed all its rain upstream. Occasional drops fell upon us as the cloud moved past. The thunder receded and the earth grew still except for the annoying giggling of Judy's bunch in the creek.

Then I heard a noise unlike any that had ever reached my ears. It was like the roar of a giant wind. I looked around. Everyone seemed to hear it. We could not explain it. There was at best a cool breeze, nothing stronger, caressing my face. The noise grew louder, but the breeze stayed the same. I could not imagine what the rumble might be. It seemed to be coming from the creekbed. I took a step in that direction, then stopped. I didn't care to get any closer to where Judy and the others frolicked. I was still bitter about how they had treated Echo.

The roar intensified, yet the wind remained calm. I did not understand. Then the noise dwarfed every other sound. I looked around me. Everyone was perplexed. Echo would've known what to do. Several of us moved instinctively toward the creek. Then we saw it: a wall of water taller than two buffalo. The water rumbled down the creekbed.

It was a flash flood. The giant cloud had unleashed its water upstream. Now the water was barreling down the creek.

Judy, Teresa, Carla, and Sandy had been too absorbed with themselves to realize the danger they were in.

By the time they understood the hazard, it was too late. We heard their screams as they scrambled from the creek. They screamed now in terror, not mockery. Then their cries were drowned out by the roar as the wall of water crashed over them. The water consumed them as if a giant snake had swallowed them. The water rumbled past.

I froze for a moment, terrified at what I had heard. I saw the earthen ledge over the crook in the river shake, then crumble into the rushing waters.

Everyone in the herd realized that the four females had been devoured by the wall of water. Downstream, I thought I saw a buffalo head break to the surface, but then it disappeared. The bulls began galloping downstream calling the names of Judy, Teresa, Carla, and Sandy. Only the rush of the water answered them. Then the roar, too, passed, to be replaced by the worried cries of the herd. Everyone rushed to the creek. The water was a muddy red and still powerful.

Then I saw several bulls plunge into the flooded creek and push a buffalo out. The buffalo managed to get to her feet before staggering away from the bank. It was Judy, drenched and terrified but alive. Someone called that they had found Carla, thrown from the creek onto high ground, bruised but alive.

Sandy was not so lucky. They found her body

hanging in a downed cottonwood tree more than a thousand paces from the crook in the creek. They never found Teresa's body. Some said she was buried under the mud. Others said she had been washed the length of the creek. Whatever had happened, she would never be seen again.

I was stunned. I didn't know what to do. I wandered back to the edge of the newly carved bluff and looked down at the water still swirling below. Then I recalled that I had hesitated to walk out on the rise where the girls could have seen me as they had seen Echo the week before. Had I walked out there, I might have spotted the water in time to give a warning and save them. I might have saved them if I had just stood where Echo had stood.

Then it struck me. I finally realized that Echo *had* been watching the clouds the week before when Judy and her friends bathed. There had been another storm cloud to the west that day. And the next morning, the creek had shown signs of high water.

Echo had been standing there to warn them in case a flash flood approached. He had been looking out for them, in spite of how badly they had treated him.

He had been doing the right thing, the decent thing, and I had accused him of doing the indecent thing by watching the girls bathe. I had reached the wrong conclusion, and that had led to so many bad things. I was ashamed of myself.

Dejected, I walked away from the creek and moved aimlessly back to the herd. I could not forgive myself for wrongly accusing him as I had. It seemed like everything I had done with Echo in the last days we were together had been wrong.

I couldn't help myself. I began to cry again. I cried for me and I cried for Echo.

Others in the herd saw me in tears. I heard them whisper how they couldn't believe I was crying so hard over the loss of those who had been so cruel to me.

I couldn't tell them I was crying over Echo.

"Blanca is as decent as Echo," I heard one of them say. "They would've made a good couple."

Chapter 9

ᨆᨆ★ᨆᨆ

A Lonely Time

The spring turned to summer, and summer to fall. Then fall became winter. The herd moved south, in the direction of the Concho River. We grazed where we had always wintered. I saw for the first time one of the wooden nests that the settlers lived in. Later I observed long lines of the bluecoats riding on horseback. They moved toward the north, the direction from which we had come. I suspected they were seeking the Comanche.

For me it was a lonely time. Echo was gone. Neither Dobie nor Prescott had returned from searching for him. Momma was aging, and her gait was slow. Without Echo, the herd was often skittish. Because Lamy had not followed us south, we did not have the eyes of a hawk watching over us. One day, another string of bluecoats rode through our herd. They looked at us. We eyed them. They appeared to be predators, but they did us no harm. Several pointed at me as they passed, amazed by my white fur. We watched them as long as we could see them. We discussed what their arrival meant. After all, bluecoats had never come so close before.

Momma seemed more alarmed than I ever remembered. "That is not a good sign. Trouble follows the bluecoats."

"Why didn't they bother us?" I asked.

"They were after other prey. Once that prey is gone, they will surely come for us."

"What other prey?"

"Comanche."

I could not believe that they would kill their own kind. There was much I did not understand about the bluecoats and the settlers. Why, for instance, would they live in squat wooden nests when they had all the outdoors for a home? I decided they lacked enough fur to keep them warm in winter and to protect their skin from the sun in summer. The garments that they wore seemed a poor substitute for a thick coat of fur. The Comanche seemed to understand nature much better.

When the cold of winter softened and plants began to revive, we started our journey back north. The old bulls led the way. They, like Momma, were aging. The herd needed some younger bulls to assume leadership. Judy and her friends, however, had driven away the three best possibilities: Echo, Dobie, and Prescott. There were others, but none seemed as savvy as Echo.

At one point along the trail, the old bull that was leading us veered into rough terrain. It seemed odd that he would do that. The new course he had chosen was hard on us all, but especially the pregnant females among us.

I should have known from all the buzzards circling up ahead, but I asked Momma anyway. "Why have we left the trail?"

She grimaced. I gathered she didn't want to discuss it.

"It's no matter," she said.

"Momma, I am not a kid anymore."

Momma shrugged. "That's true. Even so, you don't need to know everything."

As I looked around, I saw many of the older buffalo whispering among themselves. Something was wrong.

"What is it, Momma? I'm an adult now."

"But you're still my baby, Blanca."

"Your baby is grown. And, I'm getting upset that you won't tell me what's wrong."

She continued walking in silence. Downwind from

the spot the leader had avoided, the answer came drifting on the breeze. It was the stench of death. Something had died on the trail. The elders didn't want us all to see it.

"You can't hide it from me now, Momma. I can smell it. What happened?"

Momma grimaced. "They came upon three bodies."

Fear raced through me. I trembled. Three bodies? Had something had happened to Echo, Dobie, and Prescott?

"Oh, no," I said. "Was it someone we knew?"

Alarmed by my sudden terror, Momma responded, "That is why I didn't want to tell you. I knew it would just upset you."

I could barely get out my next question. "Wa-was Echo among them?"

Momma stopped in her tracks, then smiled. "No, Blanca, it wasn't buffalo, but three Comanche. The bluecoats must have killed them."

The panic drained from me. For a moment, I felt completely limp, as if I couldn't take another step without falling. The thought had been so horrible that it took me a minute to recover. I was thankful that Echo was safe—at least thankful that he wasn't among the bodies. In reality, I no longer knew for certain that Echo was alive, though I had a feeling he must be.

The rest of the journey back to the land of my birth, the elders debated the significance of the three dead Comanche. What did it mean to the future of our herd, the future of all buffalo? Certainly, it was a bad omen. If the bluecoats killed their own kind, they would surely turn against the buffalo. We had much to ponder.

By the time we reached the edge of the Llano Estacado, some of the females my age had begun to have calves. I envied them. They were bringing new lives into the world. I wanted calves of my own. The sight of newborns moving awkwardly amid the herd made me lonely. I missed Echo even more.

Although the previous spring had brought the great rains, this one did not. The rains the year before had brought a most beautiful expanse of wildflowers. This spring was bone dry. The flowers were scarce. The grass was thin and bitter.

When we reached the land of my birth, I was excited to hear a familiar cry from the sky. It was Lamy. I looked up and smiled. She waved her wings, then glided to earth. She landed at my hooves.

Lamy greeted me warmly. "Welcome back, Blanca. I am glad you have returned." She studied the herd, then eyed me.

"No," I said, "Echo has not returned, nor have we heard from Dobie and Prescott."

"I am sorry," Lamy said.

I was, too. "And how is your family?" I asked.

"The kids are on their own now. Elroy still talks about Echo saving him from the coyote. He embellishes his own bravery. He thinks he drove the coyote away, but he means well. I can die knowing he is a good one. He hasn't forgotten what you and Echo did for him. He says one day he will repay you."

"He did that last spring. Remember how he watched over the herd while you searched for Echo?"

"Oh, that was to repay Echo. He says he must still repay you."

"Echo saved him from the coyote."

Lamy shook her head. "He thinks you both saved him. He plans to do a favor for you, Blanca. He wants to do it when he's through traveling."

"Traveling?"

"Yes, he wants to see Texas. He's young and energetic. I envy him that, but I always preferred to stay closer to home. It's nice to have a nest you can call your own. It's a comfort to return there every evening."

"Elroy could look for Echo whenever he's exploring Texas," I suggested.

"He planned on doing that anyway. Even so, he still feels indebted to you."

"That's very kind."

"He's a good son," Lamy answered.

As she walked to stretch her wings, I noticed a limp for the first time.

"Are you okay, Lamy?"

She nodded. "I'm just getting old. My joints are stiff. My wings don't carry me as high as they once did. My strength and stamina have diminished. I can't do as much as I once could. I remember the days when I could soar in the sky all day. Now I have to rest in the morning. Then I have to rest in the afternoon. Getting old's no fun. Don't worry, though, I'll watch over you and the herd. I promised Echo I would."

I smiled. "I know you will."

In the days following that conversation, it was a great comfort to see Lamy flying overhead as our guardian.

When the spring Comanche moon arose one evening, I made my pilgrimage to the mesa where White Buffalo had had his vision. As he had been each spring as far back as I could remember, White Buffalo was there. He sat in the center of the mesa top. He smoked his pipe and stared into the star-flecked sky. I kneeled down, then lay on my belly so my eyes were level with his. I smelled the aroma of his tobacco. I studied his sharply chiseled features. As before, he carried no weapons. He wore only a breechcloth. The

pouch with his talisman lay on the ground between him and the small fire he had built.

"Mother of all buffalo," he began, "you have returned. My eyes are pleased to rest their gaze upon you."

I nodded my thanks.

"You come alone this year. Your bull buffalo has gone on a journey far away, but do not worry. You and he shall die together."

His words frightened me. Just because we might die together did not mean that we would find each other before that fatal day. I shifted nervously. *Will we have time and children together?* I wanted to know.

"My vision only sees you dying together. I do not like what I see," White Buffalo said. "As long as you live and roam free, I will live upon this land, as well. When you are gone, so, too, will I be gone. That day is far, yet near."

I did not understand all his words. Some words pleased me. Other words confused me. I hoped that Echo and I might die in our old age after many calves together.

White Buffalo, though, spoke again of his vision. "Your herd will go blind before fall."

I did not understand. Surely, not every animal among us would go blind. If that happened, it would mean the end of our herd. It would be the end of our existence. We could not feed and protect ourselves if we were blind.

"The earth of the Comanche and the buffalo is shrinking. There will be thunder without clouds, and the thunder will come from all sides."

His words did not make sense to me, but there was power in his words. And his visions had always been true.

"Mother of all buffalo, you will save your kind. Your sacrifice will be remembered by all for as long as the moon shall rise and as long as the sun shall set."

Much as my Momma always had, White Buffalo told me I was special in ways that I could not understand. Even coming from him, it was hard to imagine how I could be special. After all, I was just me, nothing more. All that was different about me was simply my white hide. That made me odd, perhaps even a freak, as Judy and her friends believed. It did not make me special.

White Buffalo drew on his pipe. "I have said all I have seen, but I have not seen all. Be ever alert. The moons to come will be dangerous, both to my kind and to yours." White Buffalo said nothing more.

I waited awhile, to be courteous, then stood and retreated down the slope of the mesa. The trail had been damaged from the heavy rains the year before. It was a treacherous walk, but I managed. Along the way, I wondered if White Buffalo's visions were true. He had always said his power came from me. I would not believe that. I had no power to give.

Five times that spring and summer, Lamy warned us of the approach of Comanche. They never attacked us. I thought the horned toads were telling the Indians our location. Without Echo walking ahead of the herd to warn them, I was sure many horned toads had died as we passed. I was certain the survivors had told the Comanches our whereabouts.

The elders debated why the Comanches never attacked. Momma told some of her friends that I was considered a sacred animal by the Comanche. Her friends laughed at me as they always had. In my heart, I knew Momma was right. White Buffalo had told me so. None of Momma's friends nor any of the elders had ever talked with a Comanche. I had.

The question was debated through the dry summer. The rains seemed to be hiding from everyone. The creeks dried up so that the water no longer ran. What water remained had gathered in pools, turned green and stagnant. It was virtually impossible to drink. Even the natural springs which bubbled out of the side of the Caprock diminished greatly.

Those were not good times for the herd. Some blamed Judy and Carla, saying they had brought bad luck to the herd for humiliating Echo. They were ostracized by most. Few buffalo wanted to associate with them. A pair of younger bulls—Jenkins and Hopkins—had left their own herd and had taken up with Judy and Carla. Most of the elders avoided the newcomers. The elders wished that Jenkins and Hopkins would go away and take Judy and Carla's bad luck with them. Jenkins and Hopkins were not so generous.

As the summer gave way to the fall, a troubling event occurred. We were stalked by a band of Comanches for the sixth time. All five times previous, Lamy had warned us, but not this time. I walked to the front of the herd and showed myself to the Comanche. Only then did they turn and leave in search of another herd. For once, the elders realized that I might have special powers, after all, because of my white coat.

I wasn't worried about the Comanches but about Lamy. She had always warned us before. As soon as the Comanches disappeared, I trotted over to the Yucca plant where she had built her nest. It was the same plant and nest where Echo had saved Elroy. I found Lamy there. She looked asleep, but I could tell she was dead.

Elroy was still exploring Texas. Since I didn't know

where to find Elroy's siblings, I scraped out a shallow hole in the ground with my hooves. I lifted Lamy gently from her nest with my teeth and placed her in the grave. I covered her with dirt and then rolled some stones with my nose to make a marker for her.

"Thank you, Lamy, for all you did for the buffalo," I said. Then I realized that what White Buffalo had predicted had indeed come true.

The herd would go blind!

Without Lamy to warn us, we could not see nearly as well, nor as far. Without Lamy to warn us when trouble approached, we were as good as blind.

I was scared. Not just for me, but for the whole herd.

Chapter 10

꙰ ★ ꙰

Longhorns and Troublemakers

The winter was a hard one of snow and ice. The weather chased us to the Concho River earlier than usual. The land was marked from the summer drought. There was little grass for us to eat. Worst of all, we saw for the first time a strange animal near the wooden nests of the settlers. This animal was called a longhorn. He was well named. Unlike buffalo horns, which were short and upturned, this animal's horns were longer and straighter—and more dangerous. A longhorn could gouge you from afar with his horns. This animal was lean and lanky, almost sickly. He couldn't possess the strength of a buffalo. We had powerful shoulders and strong necks. Even so, none of us except for Jenkins and Hopkins wanted to challenge any of the six longhorns that we saw.

The elders talked about what the longhorns meant for our future. No one knew for certain. Deep down, we were scared. They ate grass like we did. Jenkins and Hopkins kept trying to impress the elders by offering to fight the longhorns. The elders ignored them. The elders understood that a brave buffalo didn't have to talk or brag about his bravery. Those who did were generally cowards. Anyway, most in the herd discounted the two cocky bulls after they started chumming with Judy and Carla.

To avoid a possible scrape with the longhorns, the elders retreated westward. There, the grass was even poorer and the water scarcer. It was our hardest winter, brightened only by a single event: Dobie and Prescott returned. They looked mangy and tired. They had scraggly beards and thin shoulders. Their fur coats were scarred from battles with other animals. They looked like refugees from another herd. As a result, at first everyone feared they were friends of Hopkins and Jenkins. No one recognized them as they approached. The two said nothing. They came straight to me. I still didn't recognize them, even when they stopped before me.

"Blanca," the nearest one said.

I immediately recognized Dobie's voice.

"We tried, but ..." Dobie hesitated.

"We're sorry we didn't find Echo," Prescott said.

I rushed to them. I kissed both on the cheek. "I know you did. I'm just glad you are safe. At least we have you back with us."

"We tracked every herd we could," Dobie said. "We asked everyone we saw. We didn't find him. Some said they had seen a solitary bull buffalo wandering the prairie from time to time. He kept to himself and at a distance. Some bulls turn mean or bad. We learned about every rotten bull in West Texas, but never did we hear a bad thing about Echo."

Prescott nodded. "Not a single herd remembered a bull with a stammer. He didn't join a herd. He could be holed up anywhere in Texas from here to the Rio Grande. He could be in a cave or a canyon, or right over the next hill, for that matter."

It pained me to know he was wandering alone through Texas. I knew I had hurt him. I wanted so badly to make amends. Sometimes, though, there is little you can do. But if Echo was not found, at least Dobie and Prescott had returned.

"Everybody," I cried out, "it's Dobie and Prescott! They're back!"

Suddenly, all the herd crowded around us. Everyone was anxious to greet the pair and to learn of their adventures, everybody except Judy, Carla, and their beaus. They avoided Dobie and Prescott, which suited everyone just fine.

After a few days of rest and what grazing they could manage, Dobie and Prescott looked stronger. Everyone in the herd respected them for what they had done. The two were with me when they first noticed Hopkins and Jenkins skulking around the perimeter of the herd.

"They're not very friendly," Prescott said. "Who are they?"

"Their names are Hopkins and Jenkins," I answered. "They've taken to hanging around Judy and Carla."

Dobie and Prescott looked at each other. They seemed concerned.

"What's the matter?"

"They're troublemakers," Dobie said. "They've worn out their welcome with three other herds. They were banished from those herds."

"Only Judy and Carla care for them," I said.

"They deserve the misery they will bring one another," Prescott said. He shook his head in disgust. "After what those girls did to Echo, they've earned it."

"As long as they keep their distance from the rest of us, I don't guess there's anything we can do," Dobie added. "I just wish they would all go away."

"Maybe they'll leave come spring," Prescott replied.

"Or," Dobie said, "they'll start their mischief again."

As it turned out, Dobie was right.

But we had many hard winter weeks ahead of us before we realized it. The winter was difficult, especially for Momma. She could barely walk. I spent a lot of time talking with her. We remembered Echo and the good times he and I had shared before he disappeared. She told me things about my father and how he had sacrificed himself for me. Magnus died with a good name. His name was always respected by the elders. Magnus was always held as an example for the young.

Some days Momma didn't feel like getting up, much less eating. So, I would pull what grass and plants I could with my teeth and deliver them to her. I dropped them on the ground in front of her so she could eat. She would smile and thank me.

"Take care of yourself," she said many times.

"You nursed me when I was a baby. I'll take care of you now," I replied.

"I only wish your father had seen you. He would've been so proud."

"Do you think he would've been ashamed that I am white?"

Momma shook her head. "Blanca, he would've loved you for who you are. From the first time he saw you, he would have known that you were special. I did. He would have loved you as I have."

As she talked about my father, Momma was happier than I had seen her all winter. She seemed to forget about the aches and pains of old age. She recalled the days when she was young. She remembered being enamored with an handsome young bull named Magnus.

"I see a lot of your father in you, Blanca. That is another reason you are special."

"How are we alike, Momma?"

"Selfless—you care for others. That is why Echo's departure has hurt you so. Also, you are independent. You can survive on your own, even when I am gone."

"Momma, don't talk like that."

"But it's true, Blanca. I am old and weak. I cannot live long, but I have lived long enough. I have seen you grow up and make me proud. A mother can ask for no more from a child. Were it not for you, I don't know that I would've cared to live after Magnus's death. But you brought me joy and lifted my spirits. You will see what I mean one day when you have offspring."

"I wonder if I will ever have kids. I haven't even found a mate yet."

"You will, Blanca. One day you will. I will be gone when that day comes, but it will happen."

"Without Echo, I don't know that I will."

Momma smiled. "Blanca, you forget. An echo always returns."

I grinned, hoping Momma was right.

Three days later, Momma died peacefully in her sleep. I was sad, but consoled by the fact that she would no longer suffer. Wherever Momma was, I knew she was reunited with my father. All the elders extended their condolences. So did Momma's many friends. Dobie and Prescott comforted me. Without Momma—and Echo—I felt truly alone. There was no one I could fully confide in, though Dobie and Prescott tried.

I rejoiced when spring came. It meant we should be heading north to the land of my birth. I was anxious to see White Buffalo and to hear what his vision beheld for me.

The herd, though, was weak from the poor winter forage. We had to wait for the spring grasses to emerge so we could eat and build our strength. Also, Hopkins and Jenkins made their mischief, just as Dobie and Prescott had predicted. Three times they started stampedes. Once they yelled "prairie fire" and spooked everyone. Next they just galloped through the herd as if something was chasing them. Finally, they shook a

dried gourd, and several buffalo thought it was a rat-
tlesnake.

In the stampedes, one elder broke his leg and died.
Two calves were trampled. Besides that, I knew that
each stampede angered the horned toads. They would
tell the Comanche where we were.

Finally, I had had enough. I marched to Hopkins
and Jenkins. Along with Carla and Judy, they were
laughing at all those their pranks had scared. They ignored me until I spoke.

"You've got to quit causing stampedes," I demanded.

"Look who's here," laughed Judy. "It's the white
freak."

Hopkins and Jenkins snickered.

Hopkins sneered, "We're not starting the stampedes—it's the others that are doing all the running."

"You're scaring them into running," I shot back.
"Besides that, you are angering the horned toads."

"You're nuttier than a pecan tree," Carla said.

They liked that insult and laughed uproariously at
me.

"Is that some nonsense that that crazy Echo told
you?" Judy asked.

"He wasn't crazy."

"Then stupid," Judy said.

"When we trample the horned toads, they tell the Comanches where we are. We don't want them attacking the herd."

"Ha," replied Jenkins, "this isn't our herd. And the way the herd, and especially you, whitey, have treated Judy and Carla, why should we care what happens?"

"You're all mean."

Hopkins lowered his head like he was about to make a run for my stomach with his horns, but he froze when he heard a voice behind him.

"Leave her alone." It was Dobie, with Prescott beside him.

"This is none of your affair, Dobie. You either, Prescott."

"It is when you're threatening one of our females. Why don't you fight another bull?"

Hopkins raised his head and grinned at Jenkins. "Nobody in this herd can take a joke."

"Your jokes aren't funny," answered Prescott. "Let's go, Blanca. Stay away from these troublemakers. We know their reputations from other herds."

That afternoon, Hopkins and Jenkins abandoned Judy and Carla and headed west. At first I thought they were leaving the herd for good. Unfortunately, they returned the next morning. As they neared me, they spoke in hushed tones that I could barely make out.

"Reckon we ought to tell her about the buffalo bull? You know, the one that's a half-day's walk to the west?" Hopkins asked.

"You mean the one that kept saying, 'B-bla-blanca'?" Jenkins answered.

My spirits lifted.

"That's the one," Hopkins said.

"No," Jenkins replied, "Dobie and Prescott told us to stay away from her. We don't want to be trouble-makers, now, do we, Hopkins?"

They had barely turned toward Judy and Carla before I bolted to the west. They must have laughed at how gullible I was. I could not live with myself if Echo were near. I had to go to him. I had to find him. I ran and ran and ran, hoping to spot him. I found nothing but disappointment.

When I realized the troublemakers had tricked me into a wild goose chase, my spirits fell. Angrily, I re-traced my path to where I left the herd. I was horrified at what I found. Many buffalo were still there, but they were dead. Comanches swarmed over them like ants. They were skinning them and saving the meat after a large sacrifice. I counted eighteen dead. The power that

White Buffalo said I had to protect the herd was useless when I was away.

One of the warriors among the Comanche saw me. He whooped, then pointed me out to the others. They stopped and gazed upon me. They seemed awed that they had seen me, the true white buffalo. Whatever power I had was too late to help the dead. I turned and headed north to rejoin the herd. It took me two days to find the others. When I did, I learned of the terrible toll. Prescott had been killed, along with four elders. Echo's father and mother had died, and so had three of Momma's friends and seven other buffalo. It was a sad occasion for me. I felt it was my fault. Had I never chastised Hopkins and Jenkins about starting the stampedes, they might not have tricked me. Had they not fooled me, I would have stayed with the herd. The powers of my white fur might have prevented the sacrifice.

I was sad. Even more so when I found Dobie among the wounded. He had taken an arrow in the shoulder. A lance had sliced the top of his right foreleg, so he walked in great pain. I feared he would be angered that I had abandoned the herd. I was surprised when he greeted me warmly.

"Thank goodness you are alive," he said.

"I'm sorry you were injured," I answered. "Do you hurt?"

"Not as much, now that you are back."

I felt humbled to be so gratefully received. "I heard that Prescott was killed."

Dobie nodded. "He saved Judy and Carla when Hopkins and Jenkins ran away. Saving them wasn't worth his life."

"Maybe it'll be worth it if Hopkins and Jenkins stay away."

Dobie shook his head. "The cowards have already returned and are bullying the elders to allow them to lead the herd."

"We must do something, Dobie."

"What can we do? The elders are old, and most of the younger bulls among us have been wounded. We stayed to protect our mothers, sisters, and kids when the Comanches came. We have wounds or sprains. Many of us can barely walk. Few of us can fight."

Dobie was right. It would be weeks before anyone could challenge Hopkins and Jenkins. Until then, they would bully anyone they wanted. They were encouraged by Judy and Carla. Those two would have Hopkins and Jenkins settle scores with anyone they disliked. I knew I would be one of the first they would pester.

I stayed near Dobie that night in case he needed anything. It seemed that such a catastrophe had hit the herd, we might never recover. I was anxious to return to the broken land of my birth and learn what White Buffalo had seen of my future. But now I could never leave my herd again, for fear that it would be attacked.

I was right about Hopkins and Jenkins. About high sun the next day, I walked to a little creek nearby. They ambled out toward me, loud and boisterous. I tried to ignore them, but they planned to hurt me. One got on either side of me. They began to shove me back and forth between them.

"Stop!" I screamed at them. They shoved harder.

"What's the matter, freak?" shouted Hopkins.

"Where'd you run off and hide when the Comanches came?" Jenkins demanded.

"Go away," I cried, trying to back out from between them, but they were stronger than me. I lowered my head, hoping I could thrust my horns up into one of them. Instead, they pinned my head down for a moment. Then they hooked their horns under mine and lifted my head. I felt powerless between them. I knew no one in the herd was strong enough to help me. I felt so helpless I was about to cry, when I heard a strong voice call out from behind me.

"Leave … her … alone!"

The voice carried such strength and power that it pulled Hopkins and Jenkins from me. They spun around and stared.

"Who are you?" Hopkins demanded.

"What does it matter who I am? What matters is you're bothering her. She wants you to stop."

"You're not part of this herd," Jenkins said.

"I am now," the intruder answered, his voice as hard as the gaze in his eyes.

He was a magnificent bull, bigger and stronger than any I had ever seen. He had a long, striking beard. He was perfectly handsome except for two flaws. First, there was the line of a purple scar across the side of his humped shoulder. Second, the tip of one horn had been knocked off. Otherwise, he looked more powerful than any buffalo bull I had ever seen.

He was so big and strong that Hopkins and Jenkins actually trembled when he stepped toward them.

"Okay, fellow, you can save the freak," Hopkins said.

"Who'd want her?" Jenkins asked.

"I would," the bull replied.

Jenkins and Hopkins winked, as if the newcommer was going to abuse me as they had planned to.

The bull quickly convinced them they were wrong.

He dipped his head and started toward them. They each broke and retreated in opposite directions. The bull watched to make certain that they stayed away. When he felt it was safe, this bull turned to me.

"Thank you, sir. My name is—" I started, but before I could introduce myself, he interrupted.

"Your name," he said, "is B-bla-blanca."

I gasped. I had not recognized him.

It was Echo. He had returned.

Chapter 11

A Fair and Just Leader

I could not believe my eyes. Echo was standing before me. He was more handsome than I remembered. I stepped to him and shyly kissed him on the cheek. "Where have you been, Echo?"

"All over," he replied.

"What did you do?"

"I walked and I talked. I walked as many miles as I could across Texas. I talked to myself every step of the way. I practiced so I could speak and not embarrass you."

"You never embarrassed me, Echo. And, I never cared for Dobie. I was just trying to make you jealous. I wanted to make you like me more. Dobie's a friend, then and now, nothing more."

"I could never have liked you any more than I did

then," he said. "I also realized that Dobie was my friend, and that he hadn't betrayed me to court you."

"But how did you find out, Echo?"

"Other buffalo told me."

"But Dobie and Prescott said they had not run into a single herd that had seen you."

Echo nodded. "But at each herd they said they were looking for a stuttering bull. By the time I rejoined the herds, I was no longer stuttering. Dobie and Prescott always asked for a bull named 'Echo.' I was going by 'Battus.'

"When I learned," Echo continued, "that Dobie and Prescott were the names of the two bulls searching for me, I knew I had misinterpreted what I had seen of you and Dobie. If he had truly been courting you, he would have stayed with you instead of searching for me. Please forgive me."

"Please forgive *me*, Echo," I answered. "I should never have tried to trick you. Because of that, we lost two years together. I am sorry for that."

"Don't be. I was not going to ask you to be my mate until I could speak without stammering. Had I stayed with the herd, I might never have stopped stuttering."

"I feared my white fur would embarrass you."

"Never. Besides, you're the prettiest buffalo I ever saw—and I saw plenty of them during my journey.

Funny thing is, there's one word I can't say without stuttering."

"What is it?"

"It's the prettiest word I know."

"Tell me, please."

"It's B-bla-blanca."

I began to cry. My dream had come true. Echo had returned. He thought as much of me as I thought of him.

He began to nuzzle his head against my shoulder to comfort me. "Don't be sad."

"I'm not. I'm as happy as I ever have been. This has been a sad year. Your return will change that." I told him about the deaths of Lamy, Momma, Prescott, his father, his mother, and the others. He stiffened when I told him about Hopkins and Jenkins. I told how they had pestered the herd. I related how they had tricked me and cost the lives of eighteen. I explained how they were trying to take over the herd from the elders.

With Echo's return, however, I no longer worried about Hopkins and Jenkins.

"Let me take you to the others," I said. "They will be so glad to see you, especially Dobie. He was devastated when you left."

I trotted toward the herd, accompanied by Echo. Several stared at him, likely wondering who he was.

They had to respect him for backing down Hopkins and Jenkins.

"Look everyone!" I cried. "It's Echo! He's returned!"

"Hurrah!" shouted several, while others trotted over to greet him.

Echo seemed embarrassed by the attention. I was so proud of him. I was honored at how he had overcome his stammering—just to impress me, no less. Everyone seemed delighted about his return, everyone except Judy, Carla, Hopkins, and Jenkins. They skulked around the perimeter of the herd. Their faces wore scowls.

Echo greeted everyone who came to welcome him. "Where's Dobie?"

Several pointed to a wallow where the injured rested. Echo trotted that way, me by his side.

"Dobie, Dobie!" I cried. "Look who has returned!"

His face brightened. "I heard the rumor, but I could not believe it." He struggled to get up.

"Stay where you are, Dobie," commanded Echo. "After all, you spent almost two years looking for me, so I can at least walk over to you."

"I didn't spend it very well, seeing as how I never found you."

"But it's what brought me back. I learned from others of two buffalo searching for me. I knew it had to be you and Prescott. You were the only two foolish enough to waste time looking for me. And Dobie, you were the only one willing to spend time with me to get the stutter out of my tongue."

"You're speaking well, Echo, better than me, even." Dobie smiled for a moment, then saddened. "I guess you heard about Prescott?"

"Sadly, I did."

Dobie glanced around. "I don't see the trouble-makers that caused his demise."

"I've met them already. We didn't get along very well."

"They've pestered every herd they've associated with," Dobie said. "Believe me, Prescott and I heard a lot about them from all the herds we visited."

Echo said, "I don't think they will be much longer with this herd."

Dobie grinned. "I didn't think so, now that you've returned."

For the rest of the day, Echo visited with virtually everyone in the herd, renewing old acquaintances. He shared stories about his youth and met all the new calves. It was then that I realized his name was as respected as that of my father. That made me proud. I just wished Momma had lived to see us together again. But she had known it all along. After all, she had reminded me that every echo returns.

Come evening, the elders wanted to speak with Echo. I was pleased that they had shown so much respect to him, but I was not allowed at the meeting. When it was over, Echo told me they had offered him the leadership of the herd. He had accepted their offer. We both knew what that would mean. A showdown with Hopkins and Jenkins!

I had a fitful night's sleep. I worried about the encounter that I knew would come. I kept hearing the admonition of White Buffalo that Echo and I would die together. I hoped that it would not be so soon after his return.

The sun had barely cleared the horizon when Echo announced that the herd would move as soon as the wounded could travel. When they could walk, even if it was for only a few hours each day, we would begin the journey. We would return to the broken land where Echo and I were born.

Trouble came instantly from Hopkins and Jenkins. They bulled their way between the others listening to Echo's instructions.

"Who made you boss all of a sudden?" Hopkins demanded.

Echo turned toward him. "The elders."

"You have no right to be boss," Jenkins said as he eased toward Echo's flank.

"On top of that," Hopkins interjected, "I hear you're about as stupid a bull as was ever born."

Echo nodded. "You've been talking to Judy and Carla. You can take them with you when I kick you out of the herd."

"We're not going anywhere," Hopkins announced. "It's you who'll be leaving. You can go back to wandering Texas like the outcast you are."

Both Hopkins and Jenkins began to paw at the earth. They had positioned themselves so that Echo could not see them both at the same time. Hopkins threatened him from the front, Jenkins from behind.

Dobie limped up. "Let me help out, Echo."

"It won't be necessary," Echo said. "These two are more bluff than tough."

With that, Hopkins lowered his head and charged Echo.

Echo planted his feet, dropped his head, and met Hopkins' charge. Their heads hit with a thunderclap. Hopkins dropped in his tracks.

"Look out," cried Dobie, "behind you!"

Echo spun around and lowered his head in time to meet Jenkins' cowardly charge. Echo hooked his good horn around Jenkins' horn. With a flex of his powerful shoulders, combined with the awkward momentum of his opponent's charge, Echo flipped Jenkins onto his back. Jenkins landed with a thump. The air hissed out of his lungs.

Echo stood triumphantly over them. All around him, the rest of the herd cheered. "Now get up," he commanded.

Hopkins and Jenkins hesitated. They still moaned. They tried to grasp what had happened so suddenly. Judy and Carla burst through the crowd to tend them.

"Get up," Echo said, "and leave the herd. Take Judy and Carla with you."

Judy looked up from Hopkins. "You can't send us away."

"You're stupid," Carla interjected.

"I'm the boss now. The four of you are to leave within the hour."

Judy looked at the circle of buffalo surrounding them. "I've lived with you since I was born. You can't let him do this."

"That's right," Carla cried, "we belong here."

Not a sympathetic eye met theirs. Not a sympathetic word responded to their pleas. One by one, the other members of the herd turned their backs on Judy and Carla. The entire herd walked away.

"Be gone within the hour," Echo instructed, "or all four of you will regret staying." With that, he turned from them. I fell in by his side. We joined Dobie and walked away from the troublemakers. They skulked away within the hour as Echo had ordered. Since no other herds would take them, the four would remain pariahs for the rest of their lives.

Within two days, all the wounded announced they were well enough to start the trip back to the Llano Estacado. They weren't that much better physically, but they were certainly stronger emotionally because of Echo's return. He was a solid leader.

The following days, weeks, and months were the happiest of my life. Echo was as fair and just with me as he was with the others in the herd. He told me about his adventures. He explained how the tip of his horn had been shot off by a gun with such a long range it could fire today and kill tomorrow. The same bullet had grazed his hide, causing the scar along his shoulder.

"I never saw the man who fired the shot," he said, "but I will never forget the sound. It was thunder without lightning."

I was shocked at his description. Thunder without lightning. White Buffalo had used those same words!

Though he didn't avoid the shooting incident, he preferred to talk more about his travels through West Texas. What he saw was frightening. The settlers were encroaching more and more into buffalo territory. Along the Concho River, where we had spent winters, the settlers had moved in. They brought with them more longhorns like the ones we had seen during the past winter. We in the herd had seen only six. Echo had seen hundreds.

I told Echo that Elroy had left home to see Texas, as well. For all of Echo's travels in Texas, I could tell he was envious of Elroy.

"You've seen so much," I said.

Echo nodded. "But not with the eyes of a hawk, merely the eyes of a buffalo. And not from the sky, merely from the ground."

When we reached the land at the foot of the Llano Estacado, Echo finally felt at home. It had been from here that he had left the herd, and now, two years later, here he had returned at its head.

I told him what had happened to Sandy and Teresa in the flash flood. I recounted how after that tragedy I realized he had actually been watching for rising water. I apologized for jumping to the wrong conclusion.

"B-bla-blanca, you do not have to say you're sorry for anything that is past. I am looking to the future with you. I want to have kids. I want to teach them about the life of the buffalo so they can live on the plains forever."

The land was dotted with spring flowers. The prairie reminded me of the time Echo picked flowers with his teeth and brought them to me. He had shown me many acts of kindness over the years. I would do the same for him in the future.

The spring rains returned, and the creeks ran. The grass was sweet again, and it seemed like our lives were back to normal. The spring Comanche moon came later that year, and Echo and I once again returned to the mesa. We wondered if we would find White Buffalo. Though I was reluctant to leave the herd for fear of another Comanche attack, Echo convinced me it was okay.

As the Comanche moon rose on the eastern horizon, we climbed the trail that we had traveled together in the past. I was glad Echo was at my side this year. More of the trail had washed away, and the climb was more difficult, but we made it. Atop the mesa, we once more found White Buffalo.

"Welcome, mother of all buffalo, and welcome, great bull," he said, his dark eyes staring at us. "I am glad you have come. As long as you live and roam free, so shall I."

We lay down before the Comanche brave. He smoked his pipe and stared at the moon. Then he looked at us. "The year has been hard for the Comanche and the buffalo. We are both hunted by the white man. We have both lost many close to us. Mother

Earth can replenish herself, but can the buffalo and the Comanche? I do not know. But I do know that you will be fruitful next spring."

His words excited me, for I hoped I would be the mother of Echo's young one by then.

Next he said something that shocked me.

"Be careful, for you must protect your offspring from thunder without lightning or all the buffalo shall disappear."

Thunder without lightning?

Echo had used that phrase upon his return. Thunder without lightning had broken Echo's horn and scarred his shoulder.

White Buffalo had used the same words the year before.

Suddenly, I was scared for my unborn offspring and for all buffalo.

Chapter 12

Thunder Without Lightning

Despite the threat of thunder without lightning, the following months were the happiest of my life. I was at Echo's side day and night. We were only apart when he met with the elders. The herd respected him. Everyone admired his strength and his intelligence. He had become a fine speaker, too. He could give powerful orders or soothing encouragement, whatever the situation dictated. He spoke almost perfectly, except for pronouncing my name. I didn't care. I thought it was cute. He would always smile when he said "Blanca." His smile indicated his love.

That winter we moved south as usual, but we did not go all the way to the Concho River. The settlers, the bluecoats, and the longhorns had grown too numerous. As winter ended, I was excited. I would be a mother come spring. Echo looked out for me. He found tall grass where I could lie in comfort. He allowed me to water first. He bragged about me to the herd. I couldn't remember the herd ever being as excited over a pregnancy as mine. Everyone was curious if my first offspring would be white like me.

My white fur—the very trait that had embarrassed me all of my life—had endeared me to the herd. They had finally understood that the Comanche attributed great powers to me. The Comanche would not harm any herd that I was with. But the world of the Comanche, like the range of the buffalo, was shrinking. The settlers, the bluecoats, and the men who brought thunder without lightning were encroaching.

I was proud to carry Echo's child. But as the herd headed back toward the Llano Estacado, I felt fat and ugly. My belly was bloated and I was short of breath. The herd waited patiently for me. They hoped that my offspring would be white, to provide protection over the herd for another generation. Echo was patient and loving the whole time. To him, I was the most beautiful animal in all of Texas, even though I did not feel like it.

We finally reached the foot of the Llano Estacado. Along the creek, Echo found a spot in the shade of a cottonwood tree where I could give birth. He watched the sky for clouds that might spawn a flash flood. I watched the sky for a Comanche moon. I wondered if our offspring would be born under such a moon. I wondered if I wanted him to be born white, as the herd seemed to desire so desperately.

I birthed Echo's offspring late in the afternoon. I bore him two children, a son and a daughter. They were not born under a Comanche moon. Neither were they white. The herd was excited that we had twins. I suspect they were disappointed that my newborns were brown like their father. Our daughter we named "Flower." Our son we called "Comanche" in honor of White Buffalo, whose visions had proved true.

For the first time in my life, I truly understood why my mother had been able to overlook my white fur. There were no two prettier buffalo calves than Flower and Comanche. They brought joy daily to Echo and to me.

"Only one thing could have made them more beautiful," Echo told me.

I couldn't believe that he could find anything to criticize about our kids. "What would that be?"

"If they were born white, like you."

I smiled and nuzzled against him. Together we watched our kids chase butterflies just as we once had. Echo had overlooked my flaw. He even thought it was beautiful. I never felt prouder nor more loved than in that moment with Echo beside me and our children scampering about.

Life seemed to hold great promise as a new generation had appeared to take our place upon this earth. The Comanche moon came late that spring, so Flower and Comanche were able to accompany us to the mesa top. By then they were steady on their feet, but still curious and mischievous. The trail had washed away even more, and it was difficult for me to manage it, but Echo helped me and our young ones.

We found White Buffalo as we always found him. He was seated on the ground before a small fire.

"Welcome, mother of all buffalo and great bull. I am honored that you have brought your young ones. They are the future of the buffalo."

Flower and Comanche were awed by his words. They had never seen a human being before. Echo and I lay before White Buffalo. The small fire between us and him cast a strange light upon his face. Comanche cuddled next to me. Flower leaned against her father.

"Our time upon these prairies," White Buffalo said, "is drawing to a close. The free life we have known is setting like the sun at the end of the day. It is up to you, mother of all buffalo, to save your kind from the thunder without lightning. It draws closer each day. Only by sacrifice will your kind survive the thunder without lightning. When that day comes, the herd will be blind no longer. On that day you, mother of all buffalo, and you, great bull buffalo, will sleep together forever."

I did not know what White Buffalo meant, but he had never been wrong. I knew that I would do anything to protect Comanche and Flower. I knew Echo would do so, as well.

White Buffalo continued. "Thunder without lightning will be to you as the bluecoats will be to me and my kind. They will shape our destiny. Because of them, our paths will cross but once more."

Both Echo and I had questions. We started to speak at the same time. White Buffalo held up his hand for silence.

"Remember this, and then I can say no more. The Comanche have honored the many buffalo. Even when we have sacrificed the few of your kind, we have honored you with homages to the four winds. We have used all that you provide, the muscle, the bone, the hide, the fur. We see you as sacred, and you, mother of all buffalo, as most sacred of all. Those who would carry thunder without lightning see you for your fur only. You, mother of all buffalo, they will see as the greatest trophy of all."

I nodded, though I did not fully understand.

Echo and I smiled with gratitude. White Buffalo

had shared many visions with us. I believed Echo and our offspring had been chosen along with me for some great, noble purpose. We could not comprehend what that purpose might be, however.

White Buffalo arose and stepped to us. He bent down and stroked the fur on Flower's head. She flinched at his touch, then smiled. White Buffalo moved from her to Comanche, who lifted his head proudly to accept the touch of the Indian's hand.

"It is good," White Buffalo said as he stroked our son's head, "that you have named him Comanche. From Comanche will survive the buffalo."

With that, White Buffalo turned his back on us. He walked away. Though we would all see him one more time, we would never hear his words again.

"What did he mean?" Comanche asked me.

"I do not know, son. Only the future knows."

We arose and retreated to the trail to rejoin the herd.

Before we started down the mesa, Echo instructed Flower and Comanche. "Talk to no one in the herd of this, for they would not believe it."

"Never, ever?" Flower asked.

"When you have offspring of your own, then you may speak of it. The buffalo of future generations should know of what you heard and how you survived," Echo replied.

We started down the treacherous trail. We said not a word, as befitted the solemn occasion we had just experienced. I was proud that our offspring had shared the moment with us. I was pleased that Flower and Comanche would be able to relate this occasion to their children and their children's children.

We reached the herd, and the kids lay down to sleep. Echo and I reclined beside them. Neither of us slept well. We thought of what White Buffalo had said. About an hour before sunrise, I alone saw the Comanche ride down the mountain astride a white horse. I smiled, wondering if he had chosen the horse because of my color. White Buffalo rode proudly. I remembered how I had first found him. I recalled how Echo and I had helped him find water and his vision. In return, he had been a friend. He had helped protect the herd for years.

Our visit gave me much to think about over the ensuing summer months while I watched our kids grow. I took such pride in them. Each was special to me. I wished Momma could have been here to see them grow into the handsome animals I knew they would become.

The summer months were happy for us, and so was the fall. Twice we saw lines of bluecoats heading in the direction I had seen White Buffalo ride. The bluecoats did not bother us, but they worried us. Wherever they went, the Comanches left. When the Comanches left, those who carried thunder without lightning came. They, in turn, would be followed by settlers and long-horns.

As the weather turned cool, we began to move south for the winter. We soon realized that our world had changed. Stragglers from other herds asked to join us, their companions having been wiped out by thunder without lightning. We even ran into Judy, Carla, Hopkins, and Jenkins. They had children of their own and begged to join our herd. No one trusted them. Times were too perilous to worry about troublemakers among us. Even so, Echo took the question to the elders. The elders remembered the tricks that Hopkins and Jenkins had played on the herd. They did not want them back. Echo returned to the troublemakers and informed them that they were not wanted.

From the survivors who did join us, we learned that those who brought thunder without lightning were moving onto our lands. The trespassers came from the east and from the south. We no longer could roam the land as our ancestors had.

We stopped five days from the Concho River, then turned west. Few in the herd knew why we changed directions. Echo, who always ranged ahead of the herd to warn the horned toads, had forbidden that the reason be discussed. He had come to a rise but galloped back to us with orders for no one to top the rise. He asked Dobie to watch after Flower and Comanche. Then he escorted me to the place he had prohibited the others from seeing.

From the buzzards circling overhead, I imagined what I would see. Even so, I had no idea of the scale. As I topped the rise, I gasped. There before me were hundreds of buffalo carcasses. They were stripped of their hides and left to rot in the sun. I had never seen so much death. I felt sick.

"We must understand the vision of White Buffalo. Otherwise, this is the fate that awaits Flower, Comanche, and all the buffalo," he said. "I am sorry that I must show this to you, B-bla-blanca, but we must save our children."

"I will do whatever it takes, Echo. We must make certain that Flower, Comanche, and the others survive." I turned away. I could not stand to look at the death of so many.

We rejoined the herd and wintered far northwest of the Concho River, where we had once stayed. Echo and

I lived a nervous winter. We feared for our kids and the herd. Even so, those were enjoyable times, watching the kids grow into yearlings. Echo and I were so proud of Flower and Comanche. We were certain that no buffalo couple had ever had so bright and fine a pair of offspring.

In spite of our worries that winter, we saw no humans. We had no casualties, save for a few of the elders who died of old age. When we began our return journey to the Llano Estacado, we had hopes that thunder without lightning would not reach into the rugged country of my birth. Barely two days into the trip, our hopes were dashed.

While Echo ranged ahead to warn the horned toads, the herd stopped to graze. I was watching Comanche and Flower when I heard a noise unlike any that had ever reached my ears before.

BOOM, then CRACK!

It startled me. I couldn't figure it out. I looked overhead. It was a cloudless sky. Then it hit me: Thunder without lightning! I looked all around. I could not see where it came from.

Echo heard it, too, and came running back to me. "Get to the middle of the herd with the kids!" he yelled.

"Comanche, Flower, come with me!" I screamed.

Dobie ran up and looked all around, trying to spot the source of the danger. He knew that my white hide would be a prize among the hunters. He rushed to protect me.

BOOM, CRACK! It roared again.

Dobie stumbled, then fell to the ground. Blood poured out of his nostrils.

"Run, kids," I cried and started pushing them toward the center of the milling herd. I was desperate to hide them from danger. I didn't know where to hide them, though, because I didn't know the source of the danger. Echo stood among us, trying to keep the herd calm while at the same time protecting his kids.

"Which way do we run?" I cried.

"I don't know," Echo answered. "I can't see the source of thunder without lightning."

The air smelled of panic.

BOOM, CRACK!

"Three of us are down!" Echo cried.

"Dobie's one of them!" I shouted.

We might all have died that day had it not been for White Buffalo. He and a dozen warriors galloped past us on their ponies and headed for a small rise. The Comanche gave war cries and attacked those who had turned thunder without lightning upon our herd. We heard the pops and shouts of battle. Then we listened to Comanche cries of victory. The Comanche had killed those who would kill us.

"We must leave," Echo called. He ordered everyone toward the north. For a moment I stood by him as Comanche and Flower trembled between us. We all looked toward the Comanches. White Buffalo raised his lance over his head in a salute to us.

"We must go," Echo repeated.

"What about Dobie?" I asked.

Echo grimaced. He knew he should stay with the herd, but he couldn't leave his friend. "Go with the kids. I will rejoin you."

When he returned, Echo was sad. "Dobie died before I had a chance to comfort or thank him."

We marched somberly north. By dusk, Echo was back in the lead, when we came upon a site where six buffalo had been massacred. Echo let the herd pass by close enough to see the bodies. Everyone now understood the threat to our survival. The hideless bodies were red, purple, and bloated. Their tongues had been cut out, as well.

I sensed I had known the dead.

When Echo realized that two yearlings were among the six bodies, he walked among them. He shook his head and returned to me.

"It was Judy and her band," Echo said. "Their offspring, too."

Now my worst fear was that a similar fate awaited my kids.

We traveled day and night to reach the land of my birth. Though the flowers bloomed, they did not seem so bright. Though the grass grew, it did not seem as lush nor taste as sweet. We walked the land we loved most, but we no longer felt safe upon it.

Fortunately, the Comanche moon came early that spring. Echo went alone to the mesa, leaving me to watch over the kids and protect the herd. He came back shortly.

"The trail has been washed out. No one can reach the top now. We cannot learn our fate."

White Buffalo had already revealed our fate. It was just that we didn't yet understand it. Somehow our kids would survive, but for that to happen, it would require a great sacrifice on our part.

As spring gave way to summer, we heard distant thunder without lightning. It seemed to come from all directions, and there was no way any of us, much less the children, might survive.

And then one day, just as White Buffalo had predicted, the herd was no longer blind.

Chapter 13

The Proper Thing to Do

Desperation filled our days. How would we survive? Or at least, how would our children survive?

The answer dropped out of the sky one day and landed right in front of me. It was a fine-looking hawk. He knew me by name.

"Hello, Blanca," he said. "Remember me?"

There was a resemblance to Lamy. I realized it had to be the bird Echo had saved from the coyote. "Elroy. You're Elroy, aren't you?"

He nodded. "I've come to return the favor."

"How'd you find us?"

Elroy laughed. "You're easy to find with that white coat, remember? Now, Echo would have been hard to find."

"Sometimes I forget I'm different."

"It doesn't matter as long as you are you," he replied.

"Echo," I called, "we have a visitor. We have eyes again."

Then it hit me. We were no longer blind. White Buffalo's prophecy had come true.

Echo trotted up. He grinned. "Elroy, it's great to see you. You've grown so."

"Not as much as you," Elroy replied.

Flower and Comanche approached. They were curious about our guest.

"Elroy, I'd like you to meet Flower and Comanche."

The hawk eyed them, then nodded his approval. "You two are barely bigger than your folks were when they saved me. They saved me from a coyote as big as that mesa over there." He lifted his wing and pointed to the butte where we had met White Buffalo.

Flower was gullible enough to believe it, but not Comanche. "Momma teaches us to tell the truth," he said.

It was true that I taught them that. Still, I was a bit embarrassed that Comanche had stated it that way.

"If you were the size I was then, the coyote would have looked that big to you," Elroy answered. Then he told the kids how their father had saved him. He explained that his mother's gratitude was so great that she watched out for our herd for years.

"Poppa sure was brave," Flower said. "The bravest buffalo of all time."

"I'll be braver than him," Comanche announced.

"I'm sure you will," Echo said. "Now, why don't you kids run along and let us visit with Elroy? We haven't seen him in many moons."

When the kids scampered away, Elroy grew serious. "The prairie's littered with buffalo, stripped of their hides and left to rot."

"The hunters are getting closer every day," Echo acknowledged. "And we've no place to hide."

"There's a canyon up north, ten days' walk from here. A small band of buffalo could hide and survive there. I've spent a lot of time flying around Texas. It's the best place to hide I've ever found."

"Can we get there from here?"

"Some, but not all of you," Elroy replied. "Too many hunters around for a herd as big as yours. How many in your herd?"

"Maybe eighteen hundred to two thousand," Echo answered.

"I fear a hundred is the most we can get through. Maybe not even that many. To do it, we've got to start early in the morning before the hunters rise. If the hunters see them, they'll take off after them and kill them one by one."

I fought tears as I worried about my offspring and their fate. Then I remembered White Buffalo's comments about sacrifice. I recalled his words that those who carried thunder without lightning valued me above all animals. I finally understood that I had indeed been born special. I had been born with a great purpose: to save the buffalo.

"I will lead the hundred to that canyon," Elroy volunteered. "We must leave at sunrise so they can see to follow me. We need a day's head start, or the hunters will follow and kill them all."

"It can work, Echo. It can work," I said. "I know what I must do."

"How will we keep thunder without lightning from following the hundred?" Echo asked.

"I will," I said. "If the group follows Elroy one way, I will go the other. Thunder without lightning will follow me."

"I can't allow that," Echo said. "You're too precious to me, B-bla-blanca."

My tears had stopped. "But our kids are more precious than we are. It is their only chance to survive. That's what White Buffalo was telling us. If we make a sacrifice, our children and the buffalo will survive.

Echo shook his head, but he knew I was right. I walked over to him and leaned my head on his shoulder.

"My father, Magnus, gave his life for me, Echo. Don't you see? It was meant to be. Momma always said I was special, and she was right. My destiny is to save the buffalo."

"It is so sudden," Echo answered. "There's got to be another way. I don't want you hurt."

"It's the only way."

Echo sighed. "I don't know. I must discuss it with the elders."

"We must move soon," I implored him.

Elroy nodded. "I'll be back first thing in the morning. I must get an idea where the hunters are before dark. Then we can avoid them in the morning when we set out.

Immediately, Echo called the elders together. He told them of the opportunity for some, but not for all, to escape. The ring of death was slowly tightening around us. He said he and I would be the diversion, if everyone agreed that Flower and Comanche should be among those leaving. No one argued against their inclusion.

Then Echo asked the elders to determine the other ninety-eight to follow Elroy to the sanctuary. The elders were to pick a mix of strong and young buffalo, as well as a few older ones to impart buffalo knowledge to the young.

"What about you, Echo?" they asked. "Won't you go?"

I overheard him reply, "I must stay with Blanca." He seemed to realize what he had done. He glanced at me to see if I had heard him say my name without stuttering.

He left the elders and ran to me. "It is a sign, Blanca, that I spoke your name without stammer. It's an omen that you're right. This is the proper thing to do for the buffalo."

I kissed him, and we walked to find Flower and Comanche.

We explained that come morning they must follow Elroy and leave us behind forever. They began to cry. It was not easy watching their tears. I knew after this night, I would never again be able to comfort them. But that didn't matter, as long as they survived. I loved them too much to let them get hurt. If I could sacrifice myself for them, I would do so.

They didn't understand, but then I hadn't understood how Momma could love me so much when I was white. I was comforted by the knowledge that one day, when Comanche and Flower had offspring of their own, they would understand. We slept close together that night. I rested better than any night since I had first heard thunder without lightning.

Echo and I awoke before the kids and snuggled close to each other.

"Are you sure about this, Blanca?" he asked me.

"As sure as your pronunciation of my name. It truly is a sign." I looked at the kids in the faint light announcing the dawn. "They're beautiful."

"Not as beautiful as you," he replied.

We awoke them both with kisses. Then we all cried, knowing these would be our last moments together. I had never seen Echo cry before.

Comanche stood up tall. He tried to hide his tears, but he couldn't do it. Flower bawled. She stepped to me and wanted a final kiss.

"Watch out for your sister," Echo instructed Comanche. He stared proudly at them both. "I have one other request of you both. Whenever you see a Comanche moon, always think of your mother. Always remember what she did for you and for the buffalo."

They nodded. "We love you, Momma," they said.

"I love you both, too."

As the chosen hundred gathered nearby, we shared our final glances.

Then Echo spoke. "You must go, but always remember your mother."

"We will, Poppa, and we'll remember you, too," Flower said.

They turned and walked away. They looked over their shoulders at us. They sniffled as they walked.

Comanche and Flower were the last to join the chosen. Elroy flew up and gave his cry. Then the chosen ones began to walk toward the north. I sobbed as they disappeared in the distance.

Then, with Echo at my side, I turned and headed south, where those who loosed thunder without lightning might see and follow me.

Epilogue

On October 7, 1876, a buffalo hunter named J. Wright Mooar shot and killed a white buffalo beneath a cottonwood tree along Deep Creek in what is today Scurry County, Texas. As the hunter walked toward his trophy, a great buffalo bull charged him. Mooar fired another shot, and the angry bull fell at his feet. The bull was unusual because the tip of one of his horns had previously been shot off.

The hundred buffalo that escaped while the white buffalo decoyed the hunters are believed to have hidden for years in Palo Duro Canyon, where Charles Goodnight saved them for posterity. The remnants of that herd are now managed by the Texas Parks and Wildlife Department in Caprock Canyons State Park.

Of the millions of buffalo that roamed Texas in the nineteenth century, only one is remembered by name: The White Buffalo. A statue of the animal stands today on the courthouse square in Snyder, Texas. Each

October, the people of Snyder and Scurry County hold an annual White Buffalo Days Celebration in honor of the famed animal.

The hide of the white buffalo remains the prized possession of succeeding generations of the Mooar family.

Glossary

admonition: cautionary advice or warning.

allegory: the use of characters or events to represent ideas or principles in a story, play, or picture. A symbolic representation.

badlands: barren land characterized by roughly eroded ridges, peaks, and mesas.

bluff: a steep headland, promontory, riverbank, or cliff.

breechcloths: cloths worn to cover the loins, or hip area.

buttes: hills that rise abruptly from the surrounding area, with steep sides and flat tops.

canyons: narrow chasms with steep cliff walls, cut into the earth by running water.

Comanche moon: a full moon bright enough to allow traveling at night.

Comanches: Native American people formerly ranging over the southern Great Plains from western Kansas to northern Texas and now located in Oklahoma.

contrived: invented, planned, or calculated.

draws: small natural depressions that water drains into.

enamored: inspired with love; captivated.

encroaching: taking another's possessions or rights gradually, or advancing beyond proper or former limits.

ensuing: following as a result; taking place after.

eroded: worn away by abrasion, as from rain.

fathom: to understand; to penetrate to the meaning or nature of; comprehend.

first person: describes a story told by a character using first-person pronouns such as *I, me, my,* or *mine:* "I was born a Texas longhorn down in the brush country of South Texas." A story told using third-person pronouns such as *she, he,* and *they* is said to be told in the third person: "He was born in the brush country of South Texas."

flank: part of the body between the last rib and the hip; the side.

gouged: cut or scooped out.

gullible: easily fooled or tricked.

homages: special honors shown or expressed publicly.

horned toads: lizards of western North America and Central America, with horn-like projections on the head and a flat, spiny body.

implausible: difficult to believe.

indignantly: with anger caused by something unjust or mean.

instilled: introduced by gradual, persistent efforts.

lances: thrusting weapons with long wooden shafts and sharp metal heads.

ledger: a book in which the monetary transactions of a business are posted.

Llano Estacado: a high and arid plateau extending from the Panhandle into west central Texas. Spanish for "staked plains."

mesas: broad, flat-topped elevations with one or more cliff-like sides, common in the southwestern United States.

mirage: something insubstantial; an illusion.

momentum: force of a physical object already in motion.

monotonous: tediously repetitious or lacking in variety.

muted: subdued; softened.

nomads: members of a group of people who have no fixed home and move according to the seasons from place to place.

pariahs: social outcasts.

perilous: dangerous.

perimeter: the outer limits of an area.

pilgrimage: a long journey or search, especially one of moral significance.

plateau: an elevated tract of land; more or less level. Also called a *mesa.*

poignant: emotionally moving.

posterity: future generations.

provenance: an object's place of origin, proof of authenticity, or past ownership.

proximity: nearness; closeness.

purporting: giving the appearance or making the claim, often false, of being something else.

replenish: to fill or make complete again; restock.

roil: to be displeased or disturbed.

sesquicentennial: a 150th anniversary or its celebration.

talisman: an object that seems magical in power.

transcribed: made a full written or typewritten copy of.

traversed: traveled or passed across, over, or through.

vile: loathsome; disgusting.

vision quest: rite of passage original to some Native American groups, in which a male youth waits alone in nature for a spiritual vision that helps to establish his identity or life purpose.

vigil: a watch kept during normal sleeping hours.

vista: a distant view.

wallow: a pool of water or mud in which animals roll about.

yucca: any of various evergreen plants of the genus Yucca, native to the warmer regions of North America and having often tall, stout stems and white flowers.

Acknowledgments

All writers of fiction owe a great debt of gratitude to historians. I am no exception. One whose work was of especial value to this tale was Ernest Wallace. His book *The Comanches: Lords of the South Plains,* co-written with E. Adamson Hoebel, is in my opinion one of the great works on Texas history. I had the fortune to become acquainted with Dr. Wallace during my residence in Lubbock, Texas, and to get his inscription in my copy of *The Comanches.* I treasure his signature, his friendship, and, most of all, his contributions to Texas history and letters. *The Comanches* is one of the most entertaining and detailed histories of the common life of any American tribe.

Also of profound help was *The Buffalo Book: The Saga of an American Symbol,* by David Dary. I have also had the pleasure of knowing Dr. Dary through our membership in Western Writers of America. His works on the American West are some of the best written and most entertaining you will find anywhere.

Another helpful book was *In Search of the Buffalo: The Story of J. Wight Mooar*, by Charles G. Anderson. It provided helpful detail and background on putting this story together.

I should also should thank Judy Hays, grand-daughter of J. Wright Mooar, who opened her home to members of the West Texas Historical Association in 1995 so that they could see the actual hide as it has been lovingly preserved. Though more tan and brown than snow white, the hide would certainly have stood out amidst a sea of brown hides in a buffalo herd.

One of the challenges of writing this story from the viewpoint of the white buffalo was the animal's tragic end. I attempted to provide a moral—one of sacrifice—to the story so that J. Wright Mooar, who was a historical being just as the white buffalo, would in no way be considered a villain to this story. To the contrary, he was a hero in many ways. He recognized the importance of West Texas history and his role in it. He also instilled in his children and grandchildren an understanding of the unique place of the white hide. They, in turn, have preserved it for posterity as a reminder of the days when the buffalo truly did roam West Texas.

Several individuals at Angelo State University deserve my thanks in granting me permission to use the name of the university and the Dr. Ralph R. Chase

West Texas Collection in the premise for this story. Suzanne Campbell, head of the West Texas Collection, and Dr. Maurice Fortin, director of the Porter Henderson Library, have been especially supportive on this and other historical projects I have been involved in. I should also like to extend my appreciation to Dr. Donald Coers, vice president for academic affairs, and Dr. E. James Hindman, president of ASU, for their approval of using the university in the premise.

The Animal Legends Collection, of which this is the second volume, would not have been possible without the support of Eakin Press and the people who work there, starting with publisher Ed Eakin, a fellow Baylor University graduate. My thanks go as well to associate publisher Virginia Messer, senior editor Melissa Locke Roberts, and associate editor Angela Buckley, whose efforts all enhanced my manuscript on the way to becoming a book.

I should also like to thank my parents, John and Jurdene Lewis of Hodges, Texas. They sacrificed much for my brother and me when we were kids. I can never fully repay them, though I try mightily by acknowledging their contributions to whatever success I have been able to achieve. I hope I have made them as proud of me as I am proud to be their son.

My daughter Melissa, who was the top elementary

education major in her graduating class at Baylor University, suggested I try writing a children's book for a change. It was good advice. I have seldom enjoyed a series more than the Animal Legends Collection.

My son Scott has brought me many joys over the years, not the least of which is the fine woman he brought into the family as his wife. Celeste, another elementary school teacher, can surely bring no more pleasure to her students than she does to her new father-in-law.

I cannot end the acknowledgments without thanking Harriet, my wife. To do that, though, I must first thank her parents, Frank and Sara Ann Kocher, formerly of State College, Pennsylvania, and now of St. Petersburg, Florida. To be a fiction writer, you must have a vivid imagination, but when this native Texan went off to college several years ago, I could not imagine ever marrying a Yankee. That was before I met Harriet. So I must thank Frank and Sara Ann for rearing the charming young woman who would capture not only my imagination but also my heart.

Without Harriet, few of the many good things that have happened to me over the years would have been possible. She has adopted Texas as her home and has given birth to two Texans. Seeing the births of Scott and Melissa more than two decades ago remain the two greatest events of my life. I thank her for that and for accompanying me in search of Texas history. She was at my side the day I saw the white buffalo hide, and even when we are apart she is always in my heart.

About the Author

Preston Lewis grew up in West Texas, enjoying the rich history of Texas and the stories of J. Frank Dobie. He loved books so much that he decided to try writing some on the topic he enjoyed most, Texas history. To date he has published twenty-three fiction and nonfiction books. *They Call Me Old Blue* was his first book for young readers. *Blanca Is My Name* is the second in the series begun with *Old Blue*.

Mr. Lewis is past president of Western Writers of America, which has honored him twice with Spur Awards, for best Western novel and for best article. He holds a bachelor's degree from Baylor University and a master's degree from Ohio State University. He lives with his wife, Harriet, in San Angelo, where he works for Angelo State University.

More Books By Preston Lewis

Animal Legend Series
They Call Me Old Blue
Or How I Helped Charles Goodnight Invent the Chuck Wagon

• • •

Just Call Me Uncle Sam
Or How a Camel Born at Sea Found Himself in Texas

The Memoirs of H.H. Lomax Series
Demise of Billy the Kid

• • •

The Redemption of Jesse James

• • •

Mix-Up At the O. K. Corral

• • •

The Fleecing of Fort Griffin

• • •

Bluster's Last Stand

Books Are Available From
Eakin Press & Wild Horse Press
Both Imprints of Wild Horse Media Group
P.O. Box 331779 • Fort Worth, TX 76163
www.WildHorseMedia.com

www.ingramcontent.com/pod-product-compliance
Lightning Source LLC
Chambersburg PA
CBHW051512260626
47162CB00008B/2927